CARGOS

CARGOS

DAVID POWLEY

Copyright © 2024 David Powley

The moral right of the author has been asserted.

Apart from any fair dealing for the purposes of research or private study, or criticism or review, as permitted under the Copyright, Designs and Patents Act 1988, this publication may only be reproduced, stored or transmitted, in any form or by any means, with the prior permission in writing of the publishers, or in the case of reprographic reproduction in accordance with the terms of licences issued by the Copyright Licensing Agency. Enquiries concerning reproduction outside those terms should be sent to the publishers.

Troubador Publishing Ltd
Unit E2 Airfield Business Park
Harrison Road, Market Harborough
Leicestershire LE16 7UL
Tel: 0116 279 2299
Email: books@troubador.co.uk
Web: www.troubador.co.uk

ISBN 978-1-83628-116-0

British Library Cataloguing in Publication Data.
A catalogue record for this book is available from the British Library.

Printed and bound in Great Britain by 4edge Limited
Typeset in 11pt Minion Pro by Troubador Publishing Ltd, Leicester, UK

For my wife Elaine and all our family with love and with thanks to my fellow members of the Ryedale Writers group at the Arts Centre in Helmsley, North Yorkshire, for their generous encouragement.

Contents

New Year Haikus	1
Acts of Kindness	2
Once	5
The Wisdom of a Cat	6
Cliffs of Fall Frightful	9
A Day Out	10
Captive 1	14
Somewhere in the Middle	15
E-motion	21
Late	22
Upside Down	23
Reunion	24
Seeing is …	26
The One	28
To Catch a Falling Star…	29
Testing the Limits	34
Ceremony	35
Cassandra at the Foot of the Palace Steps	37
Sepulchre	51
The Bargain	56
New Shoes	57
Curtain Call 1	59
Meanwhile	60

Ella	61
Oh, for a breath of fresh sea air during days of covid	61
Grandma's Cake	62
One Man's Othering	65
Bottles Made of Clay	67
Curtain Call 2	69
In the Absence of Seals	72
In for a Penny…	76
The Lost Troubador	81
A Conversation Overheard…	82
The Excuse	83
All my Yesterdays	86
On the Edge	87
Rhapsody	90
The River	94
No Turning Back	99
LOW TIDE	100
A Deep Rumble in Rabaul	102
The Last Dance	107
The Race	109
Dilemma	115
Then nightly sings the staring owl, Tu-Who	121
Out of the darkness…?	125
The Riddle on the Griddle	126
An apple a day	128
Broken	130
THE THING IS…	134

That's it then	135
Indecision	140
An Invitation	142
From Hamburg to Hull Hurricanes Hardly Happen...	143
The King's Chair	149
Words Best Unspoken	153
Entertaining the Cows	154
Becoming Acquainted with the God of Light	157
A Moment of Grace	160
Yesterday	162

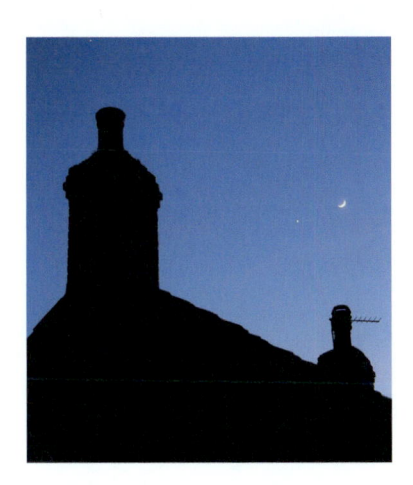

New Year Haikus

Fire and prosecco -
fit companions for greeting
a hopeful new year.

***

Burning the dead wood
of last year's misdemeanours –
a new year is born.

***

See in the night sky
Venus and the sickle moon
greet the frosty dawn.

Acts of Kindness

Early in the morning we were standing by the road out of Dublin and thumbing for a lift westwards to Mayo when a Watneys beer lorry pulled up alongside.

"Where to?" "Achill Island." "Hop in."

The driver was delivering barrels of beer right across Ireland in anticipation of the bank holiday rush to the pubs. We'd be welcome to stay with him all the way if we didn't mind helping with the fetching and carrying.

Actually, it turned out he wasn't just the driver but was himself the manager of Watneys Brewery, for the whole of Ireland. But he was short of drivers. So, there he was driving a lorry himself.

More than that, he was also a member of the Irish Parliament.

"So", he said, with a wry laugh, " the stops may well take a little longer than otherwise."

As indeed they did. He seemed to know everybody and everybody had a story to tell. So that is how we found ourselves drinking and laughing and joining in the chat, all day, wherever we stopped.

A while past midday, he said, "We'll be stopping at my

favourite place for lunch. Their fish is the freshest in all Ireland. Straight out of the river."

The restaurant stood alone, right next to the little river that provided our lunch. We ate in silent praise.

When the bill arrived and we reached for our wallets, he shook his head. "I'll take it," he said.

Back on the road and after a good deal more loading and unloading we had crossed the bulk of County Mayo by early evening and were rapidly approaching the Isle of Achill.

"I don't think it's such a good place for camping," he said. "And I know a very good place much nearer – here, in Mulranny. But I can drive you round the Isle anyway, so you can judge for yourselves."

So, that's what we did. And he was right. And by now it was late evening and dark.

"I'll just call on the garda," he said, stopping outside a house in Mulranny. "He'll show us the best place to pitch your tent."

A few minutes later he returned with a man in his pyjamas, who, with a grin, jumped on the running board.

"Straight on, Tom, then first right then left," he said.
Which took us into a narrow lane, with just a couple of houses. As we drove past them, the garda said, "stop at the first gate on the right."

Tom manoeuvered the lorry to straddle across the lane to light our way into a field.

"At the bottom of the field and over the dunes is a fine beach. And a little way to your left is a fresh-water spring. Have a good night!" With which the garda jumped off the running board, turned down Tom's offer of a lift and, with a wave, jogged back up the lane and to bed.

We soon had our tent erected and were thanking Tom for his kindness and generosity and good company and waving him goodbye.

Wrapped as we were in the warmth of so many acts of kindness, we were soon asleep. But the next morning brought yet another – the one we both remember with particular affection.

My companion, being much more of an early bird than me, was quick to open the front flap of the tent to greet the new day.

"Oh! Look!" she exclaimed, with a delight that lit up the morning and pulled me upright. "Just look at this!"

And there, just outside our tent door, nestled in a little basket made from paper napkins, were four fresh brown eggs for our breakfast.

And we never knew who left them.

Once

Once upon a time
in a boat
upon a wave
we lapsed into drifting
wherever the water willed us
I perhaps more
in the boat
while you
were the sea-swell
limbs lifted in delight
face
lit with laughter
where the once was forever
timelessly shifting shore
to sandy shore

The Wisdom of a Cat

I was passing the mirror in the hall when I caught sight of my reflection. I gasped at the anguish in its face. It was demanding my attention. Struggling to speak. Caught on the edge of its despair, I froze.

At last, it wrenched these words one by one from its throat: "Please… set… me…free…" And before I could scramble the forces of my brain to reply, it faded from view.

For a moment the mirror was blank. But then gradually my present face appeared, where it should be, though clearly disturbed by what it had seen.

"Whatever," I laughed, staring at my reflection, trying to make light of it. "Whatever was all that about?"

I waited, as if for a reply, as if paralysed by the desperate plea. From a me that was surely not me – yet as surely struck a waiting chord within me.

Then I felt something rubbing against my ankles. I looked down in surprise. "Oh," I said with a sigh of relief, "it's you." It was the cat. She purred.

"I'm a bit shaken, Porridge. Did you see what I saw?"

"Yes," she said. "You'd better come and sit on the sofa. Then I can sit on your lap and you can stroke me. That'll make you feel better." And she led me into the sitting room.

"Now then," she said when we were settled, "let me tell you a story." That was a surprise. But the way things were going I just shrugged and said, "all right. I'm listening."

"There was once a great warrior tiger, renowned as a hunter and for her cunning and courage."

"A relation of yours, I suppose."

"As a matter of fact, yes," she replied. "There was also at that time a great human hunter, whose one ambition was to catch that tiger. He tracked her hither and thither throughout the forest, hid behind trees and up trees in various forms of disguise. But, apart from the occasional glimpse that might have been illusory, he never really saw her.

"To do him some credit, he really wanted to meet her face to face, in what he called 'a fair fight'. In the end, though, he became so desperate he started digging deep holes along what he thought were her usual trails and covering them cleverly so as not to be noticed. To no avail.

"Soon the forest floor was littered with hidden pits. Several other animals fell into them but there was never a trace of that phantom tiger. In his feverish dreams she had grown a pair of wings. For all that, to do him some credit, he did set the other animals free. For him the only prize worth having was that incomparable tiger.

"Then one day, in the distance, much to his astonishment, he saw her in all her splendour, lying stretched out under a tree, apparently fast asleep. Now was his big chance. Now was a time for stealth. With uncannily silent tread he slipped from tree to tree to come near enough to shoot and not miss. He didn't notice that she watched him with one open eye. He might have had second thoughts if he saw the knowing smile on her face.

"One more tree to reach. Light-footedly he ran. Suddenly, an explosion of branches, grass and leaves and he was falling, falling until – he hit the bottom of one of his own pits."

Porridge looked up at me and blinked. "So, you see…?" she said, and licked her paws.

"What did the tiger do?" I asked.

"Stretched, yawned and walked away."

"And the hunter?"

"He was left to find his own way out."

I pondered for a moment, nodding sagely and stroking her. "Well," I said, "I've worked you out all right. No worries there."
She stopped manicuring her nails and – I swear it – smirked. "I wouldn't bet on it," she purred.

Cliffs of Fall Frightful

Once I strode without fear
along the cliff edge.

Now I stumble
as the cliffs crumble.

The only thing left
is to imagine wings and fly.

Or to face the fall.
To jump.
To have faith
in the fierce embrace
of the sea.

A Day Out

Well, it's a day and I'm out, so here I am, on a day out. The sun's not sure if it's staying out or in. But I'm glad it's not raining. Only a month ago we were begging for rain. Now we've had it, on and off, for days. Well, it was badly needed. But now the grass has greened up again. Lush, even.

Right now I'm having a close look at what's left of the huge eucalyptus that was knocked over by last year's storms. Three eight foot sections of its trunk are tastefully arranged as seats at different view points. The branches have all been pressed into service as edging to a woodland path, which itself has now been spread with the rest of the tree as chippings.

The trunk had been sawn off right at its base so, relieved of its weight, the roots, still reaching deeply into the ground, had sprung it upwards to leave its remains facing south, a metre wide dish, at about forty degrees up from the horizontal. Since then we've been dumping grass cuttings and odd bits of earth into the gaping hole behind it and, in spite of the drought, various grasses and herbs have moved in. This year, for some reason known only to itself, vetch seems to be taking over. Not just around the tree-roots but all over the stretch of land they cling to. So come springtime, we may be entertained by a grand show of purple. It could be yellow, of course, as we do have some yellow vetch elswhere. But my bet's on purple.

When we first contemplated what was left of the tree, I said to any doubters, "you just wait! You'll soon see new sprigs a-sprouting!" And I was right. I'm looking at them now. Two tight little bunches of blue leaves close to the bark. In fact, I'm smiling at them now and nodding. Yes, I may have predicted it but it's still a lovely surprise. Heart-warming to witness its refusal to give up the ghost.

And it reminds me of another grassy area in our garden which could at times almost qualify as a lawn. As such, wild flowers rarely took it over. This year, however, the mower arrived for the first cut of the season to find the entire area covered in a purple crop of little Heal-All bottle brushes – or, to give it its Latin name, Prunella Vulgaris. A herbalist's remedy over the centuries for just about anything. Certainly, for us, it was a sight for sore eyes and the mower returned to its shed.

Time passed, the blossoms died off and the mower was ready once more for action. But it advanced no more than a few metres before, behold! – another revelation! There, at one end of the 'lawn', was a pool, about three metres wide, of delicate light-blue harebells. We'd always loved harebells and had mourned their disappearance from another part of the garden some years ago. Goodness knows by what route they travelled to arrive here. Clearly moved by the sight, the mower swung into an elegant celebratory curve just beyond their shore-line.

So here I am, still smiling at the eucalyptus sprouts but now thinking of stoats. It's funny how things just pop up, seemingly uninvited. I like stoats but haven't seen any for a long time. However, there has always been an open door in my mind for stoats. So the other day I actually saw one rippling across the 'lawn'. And right now I'm wondering where it lives and remembering the time when we were relaxing in deck-chairs in the sun on what was, that year, an almost proper 'lawn' and enjoying an extended performance by a whole family of stoats. The young and the old were tumbling over each other playfully, or so it seemed, in a vigrous and sinuous group ballet. It was mesmerising. And there, of course, is the rub.

It may have been wonderful to behold for us, but in fact we may have been witnessing a training session for the so-called war-dance, with which a stoat can mesmerise a victim into stillness long enough to sink his teeth into the victim's neck and snap the spinal cord. Of course, a stoat eats all manner of small creatures, like voles, birds, rats, for whom such an elaborate tactic is unnecessary. However, for something as big as a rabbit the dance is its secret weapon.

Often, after the dish of the day has been digested, the stoat may well move into the now empty apartment, whatever the size of the previous inhabitant. Which is why I have turned my attention now from the new eucalyptus shoots to the two burrows someone has made under the upturned roots of the tree. The droppings at the doorways tell me they were probably made by a rabbit. Yet in recent weeks I have seen no rabbits at all – which is remarkable, as there are usually so many as to be a constant challenge to plants and shrubs. But I did see a couple of dead rabbits recently. Have they all been eradicated by an army of stoats? And all their burrows taken over? Seems unlikely but…who knows?

And following the smoke of that thought leads me to recent observations passing to and fro between me and my wife: "where have all the blackbirds gone? There are usually so many!" … "Yes it's strange…and there have been no thrushes cracking snail shells or singing their hearts out!"… "And I haven't even seen a chaffinch or a sparrow"… "and hardly any housemartins…" Stop! Stop! Enough already!

The sun's decided it's been out long enough, as do I. So I'm going in too, for a cup of tea.

Captive 1

His captive heart
struck stock still
like a rabbit
dazed and dazzled
by a dancing stoat.

She would not cease
her turning, forever
a shifting shape with each
new view, forever rebirthing
in myriad colours of light.

Please, please stop, he cried,
you are too many people.
I cannot grasp you,
hold you, know you.

Please, please release me,
let my feet of clay
walk their simple line
let the colour of my coat be grey.

Somewhere in the Middle

1.

Ben stands outside the sitting-room door, catching his breath, caught between crying and not crying. His heart is in front of the coal fire; between the half-heard voices; recording their shifts of rhythm and tone; awaiting a verdict.

The door opens. His father emerges, quickly closing the door behind him.

He shakes his head, as if to shake himself, properly, out of the room. A rueful smile shapes his face as his eyes settle on the boy.

"Well," he says, with a sigh, " You'll need to wrap up warm. And it's drizzling, so you'll have to……"

But Ben is already running to his room.

It is wet and dark outside but no longer drizzling. They walk quickly down the road, Ben holding his small box of fireworks close to his chest. He skips ahead, waits, walks, skips ahead, all the way, until they reach number 28. Brian's house.

He looks up at his father with an excited grin. A banger explodes and a rocket bursts into coloured stars over the rooftop.

He looks up at the sky, laughing; then looks at his father in dismay.

"It's alright," his father says. "It's only just started. "

They hurry to the end of the back garden to where it meets the allotments and a tree-lined stream, where the darkness glows orange and red with firelight.

Brian's mum drifts towards them. She is smiling.

"So, you made it, then?" she says, looking at his father.

With a wry little laugh, "Yes," he says.

She nods. "Ah, well,…..." and for a moment they stand together in silence.

Ben is already with his friends, sitting by the fire.

2.

Nearly all the fireworks have banged, whizzed or burst. The fire is gradually dying and just three of the boys are still there sitting beside it. Of all the boys in the street they are the closest. They make up the core of the gang. Brian is the eldest and their leader. John is younger and would like to be the leader but knows he isn't. Ben is the youngest and is just happy most of the time to be part of this trio.

John was smirking at Ben and saying, "My dad was in the airforce, fighting the Germans. Your dad just stayed at home, that's what!"

Ben feels the words twist in his chest and his tongue knots in his mouth. He knows it's not true. But he doesn't know what to say. He blinks. His eyes begin to sting.

"Shut up," says Brian. "Don't be stupid. Your dad didn't actually fight the Germans. He worked in the stores on an airfield. And Ben's dad was in a factory making ack-ack guns, down the docks. So...!"

John tries to interrupt but Brian cuts him off.

"So, they're about the same. Aren't they?!" John grimaces and gives in.

Ben says nothing but his chest untwists with relief. He has a strange sense of coming gently back to earth and settling with a memory of the bonfire on VE Day in their street, opposite their house, and his dad producing the only 'fireworks' they had then and lighting one. It was actually one of the flares he kept as the local air-raid warden. And everybody cheered.

He turns to see where his dad is now. He sees him with Brian's mum down by the stream, out of ear-shot, quite close together, talking. He has a sudden desire to be with them but doesn't move.

Then it begins to drizzle.

"Damn!" He hears his father say. "Come on, Ben! Time to go!"

"But, dad, I've still got some fireworks!"

"Bring them with you. Come on, John, you come with us."

Saying their goodbyes, they hurry back onto the street and home.

3.

Having delivered John to his parents, Ben and his dad reach their own back door.

"But da-a-ad! Can't we just light it now, in the back garden? Please, dad! Ple-e-e-ase!"

"For heaven's sake, boy, it's raining!"

Ben stands speechless by the door, willing his eyes not to leak.

His father sucks in a sharp breath and turns to look at him, as if to speak. But his eyes find the boy's face. And suddenly his own eyes fill. His whole face aches.

He lets go of his breath. "Oh…! Ben!...yes…well, yes, all right…we'll do that. Come on then."

They walk quickly to the back of the house, to the edge of the lawn in front of the kitchen window, which spills enough light through its curtain for them to see what they are doing.

"So what have you got in the box, then?" he says.

Ben opens his box and turns to let the light reveal the answer and he sees his mother's face looking at them through the window. His eyes flick back to looking in the box.

"Oh no! There's only one left!"

"Oh… Well…..Never mind. Let's have a look at it. What kind is it?"

"A squib."

"Well," says his father with half a laugh, "let's see if it'll wake up the dogs. You hold it and I'll light it and then you throw it as far as you can onto the lawn. Can you do that?"

Ben nods excitedly.

They huddle together, leaning over the squib to protect it and the match from the rain.

"Ready?"

Ben nods.
"Here we go then. One – two – three – and – THROW!"

The squib flies through the air and lands in the wet grass a few yards away.

They both wait anxiously as it begins to fizzle.

Then it stops fizzling. It lies in the grass, apparently dead. They gaze at it, willing it to resurrect. Unable to bear it, Ben runs onto the grass.

"Ben!" shouts his father. "Stop! Don't touch it! It could still go off!"

Ben runs back to his side. They stand silently together watching it. Then with a sigh his father walks over to it, picks it up. It is sopping wet. He shakes his head.

"It's no good," he says. "It's dead." Ben's disappointment squeezes his father's heart. Angrily, he turns and flings the banger to the back end of the garden.

"Damp – bloody – squib!" he mutters bitterly.

"Come on," he says. "Let's get out of this rain."

Ben turns to follow him. His mother is no longer watching at the window.

E-motion

He knew he was standing in the backyard. He could feel the concrete through his feet. He could smell the recently applied creosote on the wooden fence. But he wasn't really there at all. Part of him seemed to have departed, faded away, leaving him suspended in time and space, almost as if frozen. Though he didn't feel cold. After all, it was a hot summer's day. It's just that he couldn't move, couldn't speak, couldn't even hear the words she threw at him.

He could see her clearly enough, though strangely distant. He could follow each movement of her body, each gesture. The furrowed brow. Fists on hips. Her lips pursing or compressing into a tight line or opening to let out a sigh. Eyes blazing then turning upwards to heaven. Head shaking from side to side dipping downwards looking to her feet. And the tears – oh, the tears.

The words passed through him as if he weren't there. However, each move of her body left a characteristic and recognisable blot on his soul, each one adding to his collection. Eventually he might accumulate enough blots to make a map. Enough, perhaps, to guide him safely through any turbulent landscapes he may encounter. Perhaps.

Late

He is sitting in bed, wrapped in his eiderdown, reading a book, his eyes breathlessly chasing the words across the page.

A noise!

Eyes ripped from the print, ears suddenly alert.

Feet on the stairs. His mother coming up to bed. Quick! Switch off the light!

Darkness.

He sits very still. Waiting. Listening. Did she see the slit of light under the door?

The feet reach the top of the stairs and stop. He feels her standing still and silent outside his door. Listening. He holds his breath. Listening. Both suspended in the same moment but worlds apart.

Then he hears her sigh as she turns away and opens then shuts her bedroom door. He hears murmurs. Then – silence.

He lets himself breathe again. Then he reaches for the torch on the bedside table. Quickly he rearranges his bed clothes so he can lie on his stomach with sheet, blanket and eiderdown over his head, in a sort of tent. He wriggles into position and leans his book against the pillows. He switches on the torch and smiles. Within a sentence the words have him in their grip again. They draw him joyously into the fast-moving rhythms of another world.

Upside Down

I'd be loth
to hang

like a sloth
upside down

my smile
a frown

Reunion

Calving
is what people call it
as I leave my mother
in an explosion
of ice and water.
It's more like splitting
a violent selfing
into the sea.
I could feel it coming
long before it came
feel beneath her
the lubricating water
the gradual slip.
Then the loving lick
of the sea beneath me
midwife beckoning
promising a warmer embrace
the suspense of awaiting
the moment my burgeoning
weight would awake
the first crack the howl
of impending departure
ice tearing itself
shard by shard from ice.

Now I am free
buoyed up by the sea
joining my brothers and sisters
newly split
free to drift as the whim
of moon and wind wills me
free of the endless
battle with the sun
as water slowly
but inexorably warms me
drains me of reflective resistance
melts me
draws me gently back
to the breathing bosom
of my true mother.
Together we shall
lick away and swallow
distant shores
welcoming all who dwell there
back to the body that bore them.

Seeing is ...

She was upstairs looking for a clean sheet for her daughter's bed when she heard the little girl's wail – "Mummy, mummy!" – from the living room below.

She froze for a split second, guaging the level of distress – which rose a notch higher with – "Mummy, Mummy!"

"Coming, darling! Coming!"

Seeing her mother come through the door the little girl ran towards her, close to tears.

"Look, Mummy! Look!"

She scooped the girl into her arms.

"What's the matter, darling. What must I look at?"

"The moon, Mummy," she cried, pointing to the window. "She's got caught in the tree!"

Startled by her daughter's urgency she looked up sharply at the window and there, sure enough, was the moon, full and bright in the night sky, and, yes, it did seem to be entangled in the bare black branches of the tree at the bottom of the garden.

Her anxiety melted into a smile of tenderness as she slipped into her daughter's world.

"Oh my," she said quietly. "So she has, darling."

"But Mummy, will she be able to get free? Will the tree let her go?"

A sudden surge of love flooded her body. Her eyes filled as her heart beat harder against her rib-cage and she clasped her daughter more tightly against her breast.

"Yes, darling, yes." She sighed and kissed her ear. "I'm sure she'll be safe. And I'm sure the tree will let her go. Now then," she continued, "shall we stay here together for a while so we can watch her. Shall we?"

The little girl nodded.

"Mmmm, yes, that's good," she said, stroking her daughter's hair. "But, you know, the moon doesn't do things in a hurry, darling, so why don't you fetch that big cushion over here so we can sit together comfortably while we watch?"

And so, snuggled together on the cushion, they watched as the moon found its way through the branches and by the time she had left the last bit of branch behind her, the little girl was fast asleep.

Later that night her mother lay in bed unable to sleep, caught in the many branches of a single thought wheeling round in her head:

"The moon can slip free from a tree but she and the sun are forever bound to circle the earth, serving us night and day."

The One

I looked out of the window after sunset
and saw the waning gibbous moon,
lit with a creamy touch of gold.

A sadness seeped through me
and I wondered why.

Did her waning remind me
my world is about to die?

Did she weep in sympathy
with a truth we prefer to deny?

I laughed at my fanciful illusion.
She may in fact rule the ocean
but is not mistress of my emotion.

To Catch a Falling Star...

My friend Jamie was driving. There was something he wanted me to see. Something to do with cats.

"Cats? What about cats?" I'd asked

"just wait and see," he'd replied.

So I sat in silence as he drove.

Suddenly the headlights lit up a notice on the roadside.

"Cats eyes removed," it said.

"That's really macabre!" I laughed, as we passed another with the same message. "I mean, if you didn't know what catseyes are…"

"Yes," Jamie grunted…"Indeed!" With which we lapsed back into silence.

The road we were following took us round the side of a hill, which sloped gently below us to our left.

Soon the fields and woods turned into a few houses and an unlit street light.

"We'll just pull into that layby," said Jamie, as he turned

the car to face downhill. "It's a good spot for watching the night sky."

And he was right. The stars were particularly bright that night. We just sat for a while, giving ourselves up to the wonder of it. Then -

"Oh look!" I said. "A falling star!"

"Mmmm", he muttered. "Just don't try catching it – and certainly don't put it in your pocket."

My laugh died as I realised he wasn't really joking.

I didn't know quite how to respond so, "Are you all right?" I offered… "I mean, is…?"

"Look!" he said, pointing to the sky.

"Good heavens!"

The sky was suddenly streaming with falling stars – thin silver streaks arcing earthwards.

"Aah!" sighed Jamie. "It's started!….And…they are not stars," he added, as he opened his door and stepped into the road.

Mystified, I did the same.

"Then what are they?"

"I don't know…but if you look at the rooftops," he said, turning round and pointing, "you can ask them."

I turned to look…"Good god!" – and stared in open-mouthed astonishment.

"What the hell?…"

The roof ridge of each of the houses was occupied by a row of cats, all looking down at us.

"Yes," said Jamie, nodding. "I'm afaid so. Cats."

"And their eyes! They're glowing!"

"Yes!"

"And those silver streaks of light are – well – raining down on them – like – like they're having a shower!"

"Yes."

Then one of the cats detached itself from the others and in a series of well-judged leaps reached the ground and padded towards us.

"My cat," said Jamie.

"What? Porridge?"

"Yes. She is their leader."

"I see," I said. "I see." Only, of course, I didn't.

"I see you've brought your friend to see us," said Porridge, with what looked like a smile.

"She talks?!!"

Jamie laughed. "Not really. She just passes a thought into your mind – which feels like talking."

By now all the other cats had gathered around us.

Porridge said – thought – to them, "Say hello to Jamie's friend. He has always been very kind to me." Which prompted a collective purr.

Which in turn emboldened me to ask, "So, excuse me for asking but what was all that silver rain about and -" I hesitated "- Um…your glowing eyes?"

"The great Catmother of all creation, Gaia, is so angry with humans for destroying our planet and ignoring her many warnings, that she is recruiting us to lead nature's rebellion and feeding us with her wisdom and power."

"Oh. I see…and…er…?"

"The eyes?"

I nodded.

"Over there," she said, indicating another of those catseyes notices. "That's made of metal, isn't it?"

I nodded.

She turned her gaze towards it and it melted into a puddle on the verge.

"That's one thing the eyes can do," she said. But then she turned them on me and I suddenly felt their force, a powerful increase of the natural feline talent for persuasion.

"Offence and defence," she said. "And who would suspect a cuddly little pussy cat?"

"Aahh. Yes – No. Quite."

"In three days time," she announced, "there will be a huge protest march of those humans who do care about their planet….which I'm sure you'll be joining?" – she added – persuasively – and waited for our response…

"Ahhh. Yes…Of course!," we said.

"We shall be bringing with us representatives of every living creature on this" – she paused, with a little grin, then ended with a flourish – "this scepter'd isle."

Startled, we nodded once more, vigorously.

"Should cause quite a stir, don't you think?" she added.

With which all the cats as one, hissing with what might have been laughter, turned and melted into the darkening night.

Testing the Limits

two haikus

A whole lifetime spent
making marks on a cave wall
yet still in the dark

*

Perched on the cliff's edge
he decided not to test
his wings this morning

Ceremony

The little girl sat on an old tree stump, watching. Her aunty knelt by a hole her grandpa had just dug. Her mummy held in her arms a new-born baby.

"A little boy", she had said.

"Your cousin," she had told her.

Her daddy and granny were also there, standing by her, watching and waiting.

Her uncle was holding a small package. He bent down with it and handed it to her aunty who unwrapped it. It was something purpley-red and wet.

"A placenta," her aunty said.

She laid it carefully at the bottom of the hole, then spoke a poem. Everyone smiled and nodded. When she had finished, her uncle shovelled a bit of earth into the hole.

Her grandpa was holding a baby tree which he now put into the hole and spread out its roots.

Her uncle and aunty took turns to shovel earth onto the roots and to press it down.

Her daddy pushed a wooden post into the earth right next to the tree and bashed it firmly down with a big rubber hammer.

Grandpa tied the little tree by its slender trunk to the post.

"So the wind won't blow it down," mummy said.

Then everyone stood round the little tree and aunty said another poem. Everyone clapped and smiled.

The little girl's new cousin was quiet all the time. Which was very unusual.

Cassandra at the Foot of the Palace Steps

Oh! – Damn you!

Always that look-at-me flourish
on arrival!
Well -
We'll see soon enough
how well you depart.

And I ? –

I will not fall.
Not now.

Racked over miles of stony tracks,
buffetted by storms at sea,
my body has refused to yield.
I have stood erect
head held high
as a princess should.

Now is not the time to tremble
or bend the knee.
Or to die.

The eyes are sore with not looking
ears ache with not listening.

Even so,
I saw the gathering crowds
as we approached the city gates
heard the cheering
as people saw their king
only half believing
he had at last returned
in 'triumph' from the war.

Ten long years!

I heard their curiosity
as they saw me
standing behind him
marvelling at my sacred robes and regalia
as I held high the god-given sceptre –
the alien priestess of Apollo!

Words found their way to me
like stones, as we passed.
They hurt as they struck me.
Yes, I am his 'prize' -
the price of being the daughter
of a defeated king.

Oh, my dear father!
Why did you not heed my warnings?
And yes – now I am your enemy's
'concubine' –
'whore'.

Even 'beautiful' struck home.
Hah!! -
Yes I am beautiful.
Or so it seems I am
in other's eyes.
No doubt it enhances my worth as a prize

but unlikely to earn me
a warm welcome from his wife.

It made me a prize worth winning
by courtship.
Even as we were fighting the Greeks
three allied princes sought
to win me from my father
in turn for their support.

As the walls of Troy were breached
'beauty' made me worth raping.
That brutish prince of the Grecian horde,
Ajax, found me in Athena's temple
holding on to her statue in supplication.

'Beauty'! ? Hah!

Of course, there's more to boast of
in raping a princess.

The sweetest of my suitors
Eurypyplus
who valued me for myself
died defending me.

Ajax tore at me so violently
Athena's statue fell to the floor.

So it was I lost my virginity.

Yes, it took me that long!

I was young – too young ! -
when I took the sacred vow of chastity
to remain a virgin all my life
to serve the god Appollo.

He would teach me the art of prophecy,
he said. Then one day he proposed
he should have sex with me -
in spite of my vow in his name.

What did I know about sex?
I allowed him to fondle and kiss
but when he pushed me to the floor
and demanded more
my intelligence awoke.
I resisted him and refused.

This was no god
dressed as a man
but a man
dressed as a god.

Truth was poisoned then
by false rumours
that I had promised
to yield to his desire
in exchange for the power
of prophecy
and on receiving it
had reneged.

Word leaked
into common circulation
that Appollo spat a curse
into my mouth when kissing me
rendering my words
toothless -
none would believe
whatever I would foretell.

Well – the spitting was true
but was nothing godly
just wine-stained saliva
hitting the back of my throat.

Misinformation and rumours
have a way of taking root
casting shadows of doubt
over the maps we draw
the paths we take.

Gods! – Hah!

Prophesies! – Hah!

The fact is I didn't need
the help of two-faced gods
to see how events may fall.

Intelligence is enough
to weigh up the odds.

'Clever' is not a word
I heard from the crowd
at the city gates.

Yet my father with a gentle hand
on my shoulder would boast
proudly of his 'clever' girl
and everyone applauded.

Until, that is, my cleverness entered
the realm of men's affairs
when I became 'too clever by half'.

Too often I left the confines
of ritual clothing
to confront my 'betters'
in political debate
an act on its own bad enough
to earn their condemnation.

But worse it was that
I could outwit them

in argument, analysis,
reason and rhetoric.

Worst of all, I admit,
I was not – 'diplomatic.'

I would feel such an uprush
swelling and flooding through my body
of anger frustration disbelief
even contempt
that try as I would
I could not contain -

though I knew
what it would cost me
if it burst its banks -

which it did -

in screaming and shouting
tears
and ridicule -

I could feel
the growing roots of rumour
entangle me in tales
of my 'madness'
for which my loving father
locked me away with a wardress
to look after me -
and to report whatever I said

until I nearly believed
in my own insanity.

I begged my father
not to let Helen into Troy
to send her back to her husband.
Knowing him, was it not obvious
Meneleus would stop at nothing
to take her back?

They welcomed her in.

I could hardly believe my eyes
when they accepted into the city
that ridiculous gift from the Greeks –
a wooden horse on wheels!
a fat one at that!

Vain and drunk with the illusion
of victory – at last ! -
caution and common sense
drowned in a wineskin
they would not listen to my pleading
my warnings that come
the dark night and stupefaction
they would slit our throats
and destroy our city.

I ran at the horse myself
with axe and flaming torch
struck it ferociously

desperately
but was dragged away
Trojan soldiers laughing at my folly.

Stupid, stupid, stupid!

The Greeks wondered
how it was I knew
thought they were as good as dead.

Hah!

Know ? I didn't know.
I asked the right questions.

Oh, and like a sudden arrow
through the heart
I remember my twin brother, Helenus,
whom I taught so well
the 'art' of 'prophecy'
of marshalling facts -
in fact I taught him to think!

His advice when given was taken.

And he betrayed me.

Why oh why my brother
did you not come to my aid?

Well, here I am now

waiting at the foot of the palace steps.

Awaiting the logical end to my story.

The palace doors fling wide open
Clytemestra my new master's
old wife advances down the steps
arms outstretched in welcome
as her servants spread
rich red and purple cloths upon the ground
for Agamemnon to tread on
as, she says, such a noble victor should.

He is flattered
but with pretended modesty says
such rich cloths are for gods alone
not mere mortals
but he will do as she wishes
if she insists.

He makes a great show of
having his boots removed
before stepping down with bare feet.

"Stop!" I want to shout
and shut my eyes
the air besmirched
by the smell of his blood
but I bite back the word.

He bids her be kind to me.

My eyes open then -
what? kind? to me?

The ice in her eyes
belies the smiling civility
of her invitation to enter.

I remain silent and still
delaying the viper's bite.

With a frown she turns
to lead her husband royally in
- to his death.

I stand at the bottom of the steps
watching as the heavy doors at the top
suck in and smother
the smiles and celebratory laughter
until the air about me settles
with me
in silence.

How steep they are, those steps,
how heavy the stone!

And how those old men stare!
Too old already ten years ago
to go to war,
their gaze dithers impotently
from me to the doors and back
caught between knowing

and not wanting to know.
But for all the mucus blocking their noses
they can as well as I can
smell the blood about to flow.

My blood too!

A sudden surge of which in my breast
lifts my voice from me in one last
desperate shout -

Don't you know, you elders of Argos,
don't you understand,
your king is about to die!?

As am I!

As suddenly the anger in me dies
punctured by the pain and pity
in their eyes.

I see how bent are their backs
with the burden of guilt
they cannot quite deny.

Oh yes, old men, you may pity me
but I pity you
complicit in the murder
of an innocent young girl
too enmeshed in the fictions
of a powerful priesthood

and the impatience of a powerful king,
like a bird with clipped wings
your collective will could not rise
to save her -
the king's own daughter! -
all to propitiate the so-called gods
to provide a fair wind
for his avenging armada!

Fools! Any poor fisherman knows the winds
are capricious in the Aegean
and learns to read the weather
and to wait.

Hah! another pang of anger
pierces my breast
at their weak-kneed acquiescence.

I rein it in
breathe myself to stillness
and in the growing calm
I see in the mind's eye
Clytemnestra
and feel her wound
festering for ten long years
and I pity her.

I know as she knows
that vengeance will
claim her too
and I admire her.

So, old men,
now it is time
for me to die.

Sepulchre

They could hear the repeated rattle of assault rifles coming closer – and the shouts – the screams. It was hot and dark outside except when lit up by explosions.

"Quick!" she hissed, as she pushed open the gate to the cemetry, "This way!"

Before he had arrived she had packed a rucksack with food and water, which he was now carrying. He had lifted a beautifully preserved and well honed scimitar from an impressive display of ancient weaponry on the walls of the entrance hall. Not much good against bullets but at least he could attack the tangle of undergrowth that confronted them now – if he really had to.

"You'd better not use that to cut a path," she said. "Unless you really have to."

He nodded. Smiled at her savoir-faire. His old friend had made a good match, damn him – God help him! – for a fraction of a second he felt a tear prick at his eye.

They lurched forward in fits and starts, as brambles snatched at her long dress.

Suddenly she stopped with a gasp and clutched at her belly.

He reached out a hand to steady her, smiling in concern, "Heavy?"

"Kicking," she laughed.

The shouts and gunfire were closer now. Too close.

"Nearly there," she said, pointing to one of the larger edifices that rose above the wild. It boasted a rusty wrought-iron fence with a fancy gate.

The gate opened onto a couple of stone steps that led down to a locked door.

She reached under her long hair to disengage a loop of string on the end of which a key appeared from inside the front of her dress. Again he smiled. Shook his head in admiration.

A sudden explosion from outside the crematorium stopped them a moment in their tracks.

"Quick!" he said. "They're in your street and using grenades!"

Inside, it took a moment and a couple of deep breaths to adjust. When he switched on the little torch she had given him he could see a raised area like a deep shelf, built of stone, which he supposed must have been where the dead were laid to rest, except that he could see no coffins. Instead there was a blow-up mattress, two sleeping bags ("in case it got very cold," she said), a camping-gas lamp and stove, a few books and a tin box.

He laughed, shining the torch from side to side. "It's more like someone's private apartment…"

"My secret hideaway…since I was about six."

"Your what?"

"Let's make a cup of tea ," she said, opening the tin box, "and have some cake."

By the time they were sitting comfortably on the mattress, eating and drinking, he realised he was smiling again, at how they seemed to be settling into a strange new sense of the normal.

"One of my ancestors," she said, "a couple of centuries ago, decided it would be a proper recognition of the family's social position to have a mausoleum built. And this is it. The thing is, though, no-one was actually buried in it. Most of the family died and were buried elsewhere. Even my parents. They were shipwrecked, you see, in the Indian Ocean."

She sighed. "Anyway, it was decided at least to commemorate the deceased with plaques on the outside walls."

"And you took it over !" he said, shaking his head and

laughing. "How did you get away with it? Didn't anybody know?"

"Just the gardener. He used to bring me little treats… biscuits …fruit… that sort of thing."

She stood up and stretched. Then suddenly, "Ohhh!…" she sat down again, holding her back.

"Oh,Jesus!!!" she gasped.

He rushed to her side.

"She's… she's coming!!!"

*****

Twenty years later….

The gardener had been hard at work. The cemetry had been restored to order. Bedding plants and flowering bushes, even some apple trees, thrived and shone in the morning sun. A young woman with long blonde hair led a young man by the hand along a freshly mown path and waved to the gardener who waved back with a smile.

"Come this way," she said, biting a chunk out of her apple. She led him to the family mausoleum and stopped in front of the wall of plaques.

"This," she said, "is where I was born."

"No! What?! – Really?"

"Really!" she said. "Look at the last plaque on the right."

And sure enough, the inscription on it confirmed her words.

"Come on in and I'll show you the exact spot. Mother would love to tell you all about it later. Here, have a bite of my apple."

The Bargain

What a bargain! she said,
twirling in her trendy new skirt.
It looks drop-dead
gorgeous with this new shirt.

Knees twinkling with pleasure
eyes shining with joy,
keeping up with the pressure
of pleasing another boy.

But for whom is it a gain
and whom does it bar
who suffers the daily pain
carries the permanent scar

from slaving in a sweatshop
threatened by rising seas
for the price of a tank-top
being forced to her knees?

New Shoes

It's the geese again! Such a raucous cacophony of voices hurling challenges and insults across the sky, you expect a madding crowd, cars tipped over, windows smashed. But what you see as they arrive overhead is a precision ballet in the sky. Powerful, yes, but so graceful, as they sweep, swoop, rise and circle above the lake in sharp V formation, seamlessly exchanging leaders or easing into two or three separate but interconnected arrow shaped groups and back again, the whole flock breathing together until a collective decision at last to drop out of the sky stops their shouting and they skid into the water in twos and threes, prompting a rattle of ducks as they, in turn, lift out of their way.

Then silence. All the geese sit in casual stateliness, almost motionless in the water, long necks arched upwards, heads turning quietly from side to side as if to say, "Well, here we are. Just popping in for a cuppa and to pick up a new pair of shoes."

Footnote
In years long gone by, geese were shod by their human owners so that they could manage the long cross-country walk to market without crippling their feet. It is thought that some breeds of geese or, within them, political or religious sects, took on for themselves the wearing of shoes in honour of their oppressed ancestors or as a badge of rebellion.

On the other hand, many historians favour the theory that for some gaggles the custom derived from a rose-tinted and romantic view of history, akin perhaps to the periodic human enthusiasm for peasant dress.

Either way, the custom inevitably fell into the wings of fashion and thereafter inter-gaggle competition; at which time an old rivalry between geese and turkeys may have had a strong influence. For geese gained their footwear by walking through hot tar and then through sand, whereas turkeys were made rather attractive little boots out of leather.

Though, as far as we know, the geese never admitted it, it has been reported by past observers that they were insanely jealous of what they considered the turkeys' preferential treatment. Whether or not fashion and competition were thus affected, they were nevertheless pursued with such fervour, that the wearers were so badly crippled that they could neither walk nor swim – nor even fly. Many modern observers have been reporting what they describe as a 'counter-culture' emerging and rapidly gaining popularity, in which many geese, from a wide range of breeds and sects, reject all shoe-wearing customs and preach a return to an unshod state, as, they declare, "the good Goose intended."

Extract from Schumacher's definitive history of cobbling: "Did those feet...?"

Curtain Call 1

The coffin was waiting on the rollers. Simon gazed at it trying to imagine his father lying at rest inside. Then at the appointed time music played. He smiled and nodded. Yes, Schubert was right. Maybe his father's foot was quietly beating the time. The coffin began to move along the rollers towards the closed curtains. Then a gentle whirring joined Schubert, not quite in tune, as the curtains began to part, welcoming the approaching guest. Simon could feel the assembled mourners' fascination with its inexorable journey.

"Surreal", he thought.

As the coffin disappeared into the gloom and the curtains began to close again he felt a collective sigh riffle the air about him in time with their progress and ending as they clicked once more into place.

But before he could take in a new breath, two hands appeared and ripped the curtains apart. To reveal a desperate face. His father! He was shouting.

"I just wanted to say…..!"

But he never got to say it. As if on the end of a powerful elastic, he was propelled backwards out of sight and the curtains, still shaking with the shock, fought to recover their silent repose.

With wide eyes, Simon surreptitiously looked for reactions from the rest of the congregation.

But no-one seemed to have noticed.

Meanwhile

Here in the long grass
unheard hours pass
while above our herbal bed
a little spider spins her web.

Ella

"She's a breath of fresh air," we said,
as she danced and breathed
the air we had bequeathed –
and now she is dead.

Oh, for a breath of fresh sea air during days of covid

But how long is a breath of fresh air
When you're a seaman trapped at sea
But nobody seems to know or care
It's you who feed the Christmas spree?

To and fro you endlessly sail
Unable to land or go home to see
Loved ones, as governments fail
To count what you do as 'key'.

Grandma's Cake

At last the moment had arrived for mother to bring in grandma's cake. She waited out of sight for longer than strictly necessary, until, in fact, she could hear a hush of anticipation descend upon the assembled company. Only then did she kick open the door, much to the objection of its hinges, and – voila! – which she would have declared had she knowledge of French, or, in fact, been able to speak at all – there she was, with the cake held aloft for all to behold.

She was rewarded with a collective sigh of appreciation and desire.

Every year since time immemorial, on the thirteenth day of the thirteenth month the family and sundry others, known and unknown, had celebrated Grandma's birthday with Grandma's cake.

"Is it your birthday,Grandma?" asked a baldheaded little boy, whose supernatural gift for language from the tender age of one never ceased to astonish and whose habitual nodding tended to infect those who listened in awe to his words until everyone in earshot would end up nodding in time with him.

The Grandma in question was regally ensconced in a big old armchair – in fact, the only armchair – that had long since lost its legs and served also has her bed. She had but one leg herself, which was rested on what looked like a dirty pile of fleece but which was, in fact, Rumbaba, her longtime companion and bed warmer, a mangy and moribund old sheep.

As if in sympathy with her foot rest, grandma's face was almost totally obscured by an energetic growth of straggly grey hair – proof, people said, of her continued zest for life and, in fact, more to the point, of her will to maintain her dominance over all those present and several more who weren't, for whom she was the unelected but undisputed boss. It could not hide, however, the smile that spread across her features as she heard the question, a smile that transmitted itself across all the faces around her as they waited anxiously for her response.

"No, no, no, Piedish, dear boy," she said. "It is the birthday of my great-great-great grandmother – who is, of course, dead-" at which everyone tittered " – and the cake is made according to her own recipe -" at which everyone applauded.

A laughing voice from the edge of the group piped up with "and uncle Whatsit agrees with that, doesn't he?!"

Everyone fell silent as they turned to see a woman in what looked like an old blanket cut to considerable size and shape and covered in wishbones, in celebration no doubt of good times long past, pointing to uncle Whatsit's bald, smiling and undeniably nodding head.

A flurry of whispers blew across the room, or what was left of it…" Who…? " "… Not seen her for years…" "… Cousin twice removed…" "… no, no, third cousin …"

Until grandma's voice cut through the speculations with "yes, indeed, Blanketstitch, he does, he does, poor man. He agrees with everything and says nothing because he can't speak and probably has no words. Unlike his progeny here, young and prodigiously gifted Piedish."

And that raised such a gasp it nearly blew away the rest of the roof.

"Piedish," Grandma continued, "it's time you knew the truth. Your mother is not your mother…"

Which drew another collective gasp and Mother nearly dropped the cake.

"… And your sister is not your sister, but is your mother, and only your half sister…"

The gasp modulated into a groan.

"… And strictly speaking I am not your grandmother but your great grandmother."

The Piedish brain consumed and digested these words with lightning speed, his smile widened and his head nodded with increasing vigour, as he turned towards Unclewhatsit, whose own smile and accelerated nodding matched his son's.

"Well, hello, Daddy," he said. "And possibly great uncle, too?" he added with a laugh. His mother/sister burst into tears.

And Piedish said, "Let's cut the cake and hope we don't break too many teeth."

One Man's Othering

To own and inhabit
that desirable word, "othered,"
demanded a savage
amputation of "m" from "mothered"
before it stole
the "s" in "soul"
to possess it entirely with "smothered".

Painting by Jake Powley

Bottles Made of Clay

We have been listening
and watching
in our appointed places
on shelves and tables
indoors and out
secretly in dark corners
brazenly unafraid in full view
catching whispers
tiny wreathes of mist
drifting from mouth to mouth
the tell-tale beating of hearts
the sounds of blood's brush
on capillary walls
little variations in beads of sweat
their size smell taste
stories of uneasy minds
various levels of joy
and thus unafraid
we have been filled
with the subtle juices
of human nature
and are ready now to depart.

We have gathered at our
appointed meeting place
at the appointed time
watching and waiting

for the promised collection
with our precious cargo.

How few of us are left!

We huddle together
uncertain of our future
already missing
the daily titillation
of delectable new flavours
anxious now
glancing to right and left
and upwards
wondering if this is really
the right time and place
or are we to be left here
functionless in this
liminal space
forever standing
in the rising heat
until our sides crack
our carefully sequestered secrets
flit into thin air?

But now something new
quivers in the air.

We are singing!

Curtain Call 2

The curtains closed. The end of act one. The applause was so enthusiastic no-one noticed the theatre was still in darkness. Then a single hard-edged circle of light hit the curtains where they met. A hand appeared and pulled them apart. A man in a black dinner jacket and bow tie stepped through them. The theatre manager. He waited for silence – which arrived like surf ebbing from a pebble beach.

He coughed.

"Ladies and gentlemen …" He paused as if the words were too heavy to utter "… I have to inform you …" he shut his eyes and shook his head in what looked like defeat "… that the performance of the play tonight will not be completed … It ends now … with the end of act one…" He paused and seemed unable to find the words "…In fact, the theatre …" he coughed again ".. the theatre itself will be closed until further notice."

The audience gasped, then sat in stunned silence.

At the end of one row in the stalls – he always sat at the end, near the front, on stage right – Max turned to his companion and whispered, "It's happening. Get ready." She nodded.

"When the house lights come back on," the Manager continued, "please leave the auditorium quietly. On the way out you will be asked to fill in a form before being allowed to leave the foyer." He frowned and took a deep breath. "I am further instructed to inform you that all theatres are being closed …" Another gasp "…to be purged of the … 'dangerous illusions and delusions with which they infect our society and distort life in our beloved country.' "

He gestured helplessly with his hands, as if to disown the words, to apologise for repeating them. But after a moment's struggle he added with as much comradely force as he could muster, "my dear friends, loyal friends of this theatre, I advise you to take care with how you answer the questions you will be asked and … I hope with all my heart we'll meet here again …soon." He bowed his head and as he disappeared behind the curtain, the house lights came on.

Max had his mobile in his hand. As people stood murmuring and shuffling uncertainly towards the exits, Max pressed a button and stood up. Suddenly the place was plunged once more into darkness.

In the confusion Max and his companion made their way quickly to a little door to the right of the stage and which led them below the stage itself; then down a narrow corridor and into a room no-one visited but which housed a collection of costumes. He could see by the light of their torches a few others were already there. They nodded silently as Max entered. They were all changing into police uniforms.

"How long have we got?" he asked the theatre's chief technician.

"About ten minutes."

"Is everyone here?"

"Yes. Everyone. And we're ready to go."

"Very well. Well done everyone. We'll meet tomorrow as planned. Meanwhile keep out of sight – and though we're dressed like police try not to be dragooned into doing their work. So – once more unto the sewers, my friends !"

At which they filed through another door behind a bank of costumes and left the theatre for no-one knew how long.

In the Absence of Seals

In the absence of otters
We'd settle for a seal
But the one we see
Is belly up briefly on the surface
As if bathing in the sun
Except there is no sun
Just roiling clouds and rain
And wind whipping up the waves.
Dramatic enough in themselves
But not what we are looking for.

The seal arches its back, rolls over,
Dives down and into the deep.
So in the absence of seals
We dream of dolphins and whales
Of Ness bred monsters from the deep.
A fish-farmed salmon would do.

But look!
A shag on a rock -
No, no, that's a cormorant
Hanging its wings out to dry -
A great northern diver diving
Shearwaters victory rolling
Through the spray.
A raft of guillemots
Or are they razor bills ?
Too far to see the difference.

And look at that!
Gannets, glorious gannets
Their umber necks
Shorter, less sinuous
Than shags or cormorants
Firmly arched,
Silently resting on the water
Seemingly unconcerned with food
But beware unwary fish below
For when they take off
On their six foot wings
Circle upwards to a hundred feet -
Oh, if only they'd do it now! -
With wings folded back
They hurtle downwards
Their blue tinted bills
Thrusting forward
Dive-bombing into the sea.

Oh, but where are the puffins
And where oh where are
The rapturous raptors
We yearn for
The sea eagles and ospreys?
The goldies! -
A common buzzard would do.

But we are hardy folk
Well used to enjoying
What little presents itself
While yearning for more

Patiently waiting and watching.
In the absence of eagles
Funny to think that a sparrow now
Perched on our bow
Would be cause for equal delight.

Then, oh joy!
Only a day from the end of our voyage
Puffins galore
Tumbling from their burrows
Bobbing and plunging.
Woe betide anyone bashed
By their colourful beaks.

Then eagles!
Not any old eagle but -
Goldies!
Four of them,for heavens sake,
Circling above the cliffs
Being harried by gulls
Seemingly unruffled
Majestic.

Then we slow down in a bay
And there, behold ! –
A beach full of seals
Two hundred or more
Massed together in a long line
On the edge of the shore
Busily moulting.

Oh and look, over the bow
As we cream homewards
Here come the bottlenosed dolphins
Cavorting over and under our wave -
A fitting farewell
With which to celebrate
Our last supper at sea.

In for a Penny...

Gladys was already in the front garden picking spring flowers when Malcolm opened his front gate and turned right, into the lane, on his way to work.

She looked up and saw him as he approached, at the same time as he saw her.

He hesitated. She smiled.

"Ah!" he said. "Errm... Well now... " as he came to a halt in front of her gate... "good morning!"

"Good morning," she replied, smiling. A pause.

"Errm..yes...well now..." said Malcolm at last, looking at his feet. Then – decisively – he looked up again with a smile.

"Yes," he said, firmly punctuating the thought with another nod. "Welcome to Penny Lane!"

"Thank you," she replied, "I -er..."

"Must dash!" said Malcolm. "Train to catch!"

And dash he did.

Gladys watched him, her smile twitching her eybrows quizzically, as he diminished into the distance.

The next morning Malcolm could see Gladys was in her garden again. She was on her knees, plucking weeds from amongst the flowers, so didn't see him until he stopped at her gate, paused, licked his lips, nodded and, not wanting to startle her, said in a hushed voice, "Errm ... hello?...er ...good morning?"

She looked up and smiled as she eased herself upright. "Hello again," she said. "And yes, it is a good morning."

"Errm…yes…well…er…yesterday…" said Malcolm, "…you see…"

"Yes? Yesterday?"

"Well, you see – foolish of me – but..ahm...I didn't introduce myself…so…er…so, I'm Malcolm," he said.

"Well," laughed Gladys, " neither did I. So…Good morning, Malcolm. I'm Gladys," and she gave a little curtsy. "Nice to meet you."

Malcolm nodded. "Well," he said, "Must dash...!"

"Train to catch?" said Gladys.

He laughed. "Yes...well...er...goodbye."

A few days later there she was again, coming down the garden path just as Malcolm hove into view. As she raised her hand in greeting, her foot caught on the edge of a flagstone and she staggered forward, dropping her secateurs.

"Damn!" she said.

"I say!" said Malcolm, coming to an abrupt halt. "Are you all right?"

"Yes, yes...thanks... I'm OK!" she replied, shaking herself with an exasperated sigh. "I told the landlord about this path. It's a death trap, I said. But he just shrugged and smirked – the stupid man!"

"Oh! Yes! He won't do anything! He just collects the rent!" Malcolm paused a moment, shocked by the strength of his feelings.

"Well!" he continued, looking at his feet and shaking his head. "Look... errm...why don't I fix it for you? I could pop in when I come back from work and re-set the -er- recalcitrant flag for you," he said, nodding again. "Yes"

"That is kind of you! Thank you. I'll see you later then." But Malcolm didn't move. So she added brightly: "Must dash?"

"Ah! Yes," he laughed.

That evening he rolled up his sleeves and reset the whole path for her, while she regaled him with tea and cake.

And as he left, "Ah – look, er... Gladys," he said, "any time ... any time you need help, just ...ask."

So it was that – weather permitting – their morning exchanges grew warmer and more relaxed. She would bring her morning tea out to await his arrival, while he would leave a few minutes earlier so they could have a proper chat.

And so it was that Gladys readily accepted his offer of help. Indeed, she found plenty for him to do: creaking floorboards; leaking gutters; a dead bird in the chimney; changing all the light bulbs to LEDs; and fitting new taps in the bathroom, which meant finding the mains water stopcock in the basement, which he discovered to be completely taken over by spiders and their interwoven webs. So he offered to clean them all out – an offer Gladys hotly refused, with a passionate defence of biodiversity.

Then Gladys invited him to dinner.

"I'll bring the wine," he said. "What do you fancy?"

"Pinot Grigio would be lovely. Thanks."

Actually, Malcolm wasn't all that keen on wine but he loved whiskey. So he brought a bottle of his favourite whiskey as well.

"Oh wonderful," exclaimed Gladys. "Glenfiddich! Even better!"

"Though I do like exploring all the other 'Glens', " said Malcolm with a laugh. And, after a delicious dinner, they thoroughly explored Glenfiddich's smooth charms.

A few days later, Gladys gave him another job, though she blushed in asking.

"It's so silly," she said. "I tripped over the rug in my bedroom and fell onto the bed and broke one of its legs."

In the bedroom she said, "I brought up the toolbox."

"Excellent!" said Malcolm. "We'll soon fix that."

"I'll leave you to it, then."

It didn't take Malcolm long to fit the leg back in place and, indeed, to reinforce it. He was just straightening himself out when Gladys returned carrying a whiskey bottle (Glen Grant, this time) and two glasses and, as Malcolm saw to his astonishment as he turned to greet her, she was dressed only in her nightie.

"Ah!" he said. "Well now...." He smiled admiringly, if coyly, but remained motioinless.

"Well now what?" she asked. "I thought we should thoroughly test your handiwork, don't you think? And afterwards have a nightcap or two of Glen Grant."

"That...er... sounds like an excellent idea, he said, "...but... you see..." he cleared his throat..."I don't have any pyjamas."

"Really!!??" – struggling with her laughter. She settled the bottle and glasses carefully on the bedside table – and slipping out of her nightie, said, "neither have I," with which she climbed into the bed.

Malcolm paused a moment in contemplation then nodded and said, "Right! Splendid!" and proceeded to undress, carefully folding each item of clothing on to the seat of a chair and hanging his trousers over its back.

Then finally he folded himself into bed, whispering, "To the glens, to the glens!"

A long time later she poured them a dram each of Glen Grant as a nightcap and eventually they fell asleep.

Next morning Gladys got up early, showered, ate breakfast and left the house.

Malcolm didn't get up because he was dead.

He was only discovered some days later because the landlord had let himself in to demand the grossly overdue rent.

Gladys was nowhere to be found. And where had all those spiders come from?

It remained, as the national press dubbed it, "The Mystery of Pound House Cottage in Penny Lane".

The Lost Troubador

My promised song
will go unheard
I can't remember
a single word.

My mandolin
has a broken string
and I have forgotten
how to sing.

A Conversation Overheard…

On a subject entirely befitting
for two ladies to discuss
while sitting and knitting
together on a bus

"I wonder", said Mrs Sheep to Mrs Cow,
"what do you like to eat for lunch?"
"Oh, Mrs Sheep", said Mrs Cow,
"what I like best is to munch a bunch of grass
dipped in custard."

Then Mrs Cow asked Mrs Sheep,
"what do you prefer, would you say?"
"Oh, Mrs Cow," said Mrs Sheep,
"my favourite is a bale of hay
mixed with mustard."

"But," said Mrs Sheep, "I can't begin
to think how you make your custard."
"Oh," said Mrs Cow, "I buy it in a tin."
"Ah, yes," said Mrs Sheep with a baaa,
"And I get my mustard from a jar."

The Excuse

There we were, Cyril, Johnny and me, in Johnny's open-top, two-seater MG. Johnny and Cyril were in the front, while I lounged elegantly across the back, just about fitting in with the bags and the folded back canvas roof. The sun was shining. It was so warm we were grateful for the breeze we were making as we rattled westwards along the 303, singing full throttle in praise of women.

We'd all been on leave in London to see our girlfriends and were now on the way back to Dartmouth. ETA sixish pip emma. Deadline midnight. Thereafter, big trouble. But we were already in the hills not far from Exeter, well on time, and eating apples supplied by Johnny's girl.

Going uphill no-one else seemed to be going our way, though plenty were belting along on the other side and – Jesus!! – Look out! – over the brow, overtaking, in the middle of the road, a car, driving straight at us – for God's sake!

Both cars swerved to their left. Too late. The car hit our righthand rear end and flipped it upwards and over, catapulting me and my apple into a graceful arc, in which, I was told later, I completed two perfect somersaults, on my way many metres up the road and into a hedge, while the cars behind the culprit slammed on their brakes.

When I regained consciousness I found myself lying on the grass verge surrounded by people peering at me anxiously. "Thank god", someone said. "We thought you were dead".

"You gave us a bit of a fright", said Johnny.

"You should have seen them, these two," someone else said. "It was crazy. The car was upside down on top of them and they just lifted it off and scrambled out – unharmed, for god's sake!"

After all the kerfuffle of police, witnesses, the ambulance, the hospital at Exeter, nurses, x-rays, the doctor said, "you're fairy godmother must have been with you. Nothing broken! You can go."

It was already past midnight but Johnny's father, who lived only an hour away, had driven to the rescue and agreed, after some argument, to drive us forthwith to Dartmouth.

We'd already telephoned the College to explain what had happened, so there was no reason for him to hang around. "I'll be off then," he said. "Got a busy day. All right? Good lads. I'll see to the car. Good night – and good luck! " And off he drove.

As we trudged through the entrance lobby, our relief to be back in one piece faded as the petty officer on duty greeted us with a grim smile. "The Officer of the Watch wants to see you."

"Really?" "Really," he said. "Now!"

As one we dropped our bags and scuttled down the corridor to his office. At the door we straightened our backs and knocked.

"Enter!" and our hearts sank as we remembered who was on duty that night. We entered and stood in a row to attention. He stared at us in silence.

"Late!" he said at last, his tone leaving us in no doubt of the seriousness of our crime. He paused. "Not just late but very late." Another pause.

However tired we may have been we were alarmingly awake now. We knew he was a stickler and strict but surely – but no! The hailstorm of words hit us straight in the eyes. Shocked rigid with disbelief we let our senses be battered until at last I found myself saying with a frightening amount of indignation, "but, sir, we explained on the telephone–"

"That's no excuse! Your planning should have included due allowance for such an event!"

As one our jaws dropped at the absurdity of this proclamation but closed again as our collective inner voice advised us to say no more. Instead we all stood in silent but electric contemplation until at last he said, with an explosive sigh, "Dismiss!"

And with that the matter was forever closed.

All my Yesterdays

A week ago yesterday was my birthday. So now my sack strains at the seams with 86 years plus a week's worth of yesterdays. I can feel them wriggle and shuffle, whisper or shout, nudge or shove and as quickly pop or bang or simply dissolve into a dew before I can thrust a hand in to haul them out.

It's quite impossible most of the time on my couch to lie, in comfort, or to recollect anything in tranquility, because my damned sack keeps wriggling, huffing, puffing, popping and banging, or, just as bad, sinking into a deadly hush, playing possum, either way knocking the wheels off my trains of thought.

It doesn't deal in diaries or dates, specific times, places, events and only now and then anything like a clear-cut memory. The hands of the clock dance erratically to its tune.

On the Edge

2017: A bombing raid by the Saudis over Yemen. Shock waves barely a whisper as they awoke a memory.

Bottom left-hand drawer. A little tin rattling with redundant studs for shirts and wing collars, cufflinks and – ah yes! He found it. A blue and gold metal tie-clip. He laughed. To curb rebellious mufti ties.

1958: Aden. That's where his tie-clip took him. His ship's voyage around the world, showing the flag, began in Portsmouth. But not quite as expected. It left earlier than planned. To back-up the Americans in Lebanon.

The flight deck was turned into a lorry park. Covered with ringbolts. Soldiers and marines found their billets below. Armoured vehicles were hoisted on board. He was on deck guiding the crane driver with a flourish of hand signals.

He warmed to the purposeful bustle. The efficient speed with which they all worked. The friendly rapport between him and the man controlling the crane.

They were going to Lebanon!

But he didn't really know why.

By the time they arrived, the crisis in Lebanon – whatever it was – was over. The Americans were going home. So his ship was diverted to Cyprus, where the soldiers and vehicles disembarked to join British forces already there. To fight EOKA.

So now he spent a few days on patrol. To stop and search fishing boats. For weapons being shipped to EOKA fighters. He never found any. But he enjoyed friendly exchanges with the fishermen. Once he was even offered a cup of hot cocoa.

Makarios and Grivas were familiar names. But he didn't really know what the fighting was about.

The ship resumed its identity as an aircraft carrier and sailed through the Suez Canal, recently reopened after being blocked by the Egyptians. In the 1956 Suez crisis.

On the bridge, the Captain explained how pressures acting upon a ship in canals can sheer it from one side to the other. Or pull it deeper in the water, depending on its speed and weight. How the stern wave can grow in size and speed. Even overtake the ship itself. An image that quietly haunted him.

1956: When the attack on Egypt was announced on the radio he and his fellow cadets gathered excitedly beneath the radio's extension speaker mounted on the common-room wall. There was a new fervour to their listening. The way they cheered. Seemingly different people to those who rushed in each week to listen to the Goon Show. Did someone actually shout, go on, blow up the bloody wogs? He couldn't be sure later. But the air crackled with aggression. He felt the subliminal tug of an innate distrust of the mob. Found himself backing off. Without really knowing why. While they cheered. Without knowing why exactly. Or what for.

1958: Even then, sailing down the canal, he hadn't really known what a humiliating fiasco the Suez crisis had been. How badly it had damaged Britain's reputation in the world.

Disgorged from the canal they sailed straight to Aden, built in the crater of an extinct volcano. Surrounded by bare jagged hills. Now the capital of a British colony.

The army stationed there had organised a swimming gala. They had invited the ship's company to enter a team of its own. He was one of that team. The pool was high above the old town. Officers in hot-weather kit and ladies in flowery dresses sat beneath a canopy, sheltering from the sun. They drank cold drinks and applauded politely. As the ship's team won nearly every event.

As one after another of their team was presented with a prize, his excitement at winning faded. By the time he received his tie clip and cuff links he felt embarrassed. It didn't feel fair to have won.

Their visit was supposed to be a show of strength in support of the army. To impress the local population, not the soldiers. They were the ones who had to deal with the riots. The explosions. The general strike. The state of emergency. That his ship was shortly going to leave them with. As it sailed eastwards. Showing the flag.

But he didn't really know why the army was there. And wondered if anyone did, really.

Rhapsody

Chatter chatter
cups and glasses clatter
chatter chatter
the maddest of mad-hatters
clog-dances
clatter clatter
the tablecloth to tatters

no wonder the dormice take cover
in their teapots

stop! stop!
what are you thinking?!
the tea is not for drinking!

The queen of hearts
propelled by too many tarts
swings her mallet with a whoop
and another hedgehog departs
through a hoop

several fine ladies on horses
have eaten too many courses
and fall off in a swoon

hold my hand
sings a young girl

let me play among the stars

off with her head!
off with her head!

and a flurry of hedgehogs
are malleted to the moon
and even as far as
Jupiter and Mars

where there's nothing to eat
no not even dry bread
and certainly no butter
and wherever you tread
you sink into heaps
of technological clutter

nothing really matters
the young girl sings
to me

go back to school
you little fool!

as for the owl
and the pussy-cat
their pea-green boat
is no longer afloat

the pig by the wood
has eaten more than he should

and the price of his ring
has risen astronomically

ah! but the flavoursome
aroma of his crackling
increases his worth gastronomically

too late
my time has come
sings the girl
goodbye everybody
I've got to go

go to bed!
go to bed!

I don't want to die
she sings
I sometimes wish
I'd never been born at all

how is it that a girl of thirteen
can sing those words
with such feeling
as if her heart
is beyond all healing

Xanadu oh Xanadu!
the pleasure dome
we called our home
was but a drug-filled dream

no song can redeem

wake up!
wake up!

for us she sings
for us she is weeping
for us the alarm bell rings
while we've been sleeping

wake up!
wake up!

before her tears swell
into an angry sea
of sons and daughters

and together we fall
owl, pussycat Xanadu and all
into the roughest of waters
because we have failed
and sailed
too close to the wind

at some other time
in some other land
someone may uncover us
two trunkless legs of stone
in the sand.

The River

In the film "The Magnificent Seven", seven gunslingers have been hired to protect a Mexican village from a viscious gang of bandits. They are badly outnumbered. Before the battle commences one of them is asked why he came.

He replied: "It's like this fellow I knew in El Paso. One day, he just took all his clothes off and jumped in a mess of cactus. I asked him that same question, 'Why?'

"And?"

"He said, 'It seemed like a good idea at the time.' "

Ironically, I saw that film in the summer of 1961 in a little cinema in Dartmouth, South Devon. It was at the foot of the hill on top of which sat the Britannia Royal Naval College, into which I had marched as a new officer cadet in 1954 when I was sixteen. So here I was again, having left the navy after five years, working now as a barman in the Castle Hotel and waiting for the 'A' level results that would take me to University.

So, had I at 16 jumped naked into a cactus bush that was so uncomfortable I had to pull myself out of it five years later? Was it a bad idea at the time?

No. It was not. It was a good idea.

So how did it find its way into my head so emphatically in the first place?

No-one in my family had ever been in any of the armed services. Not even during the two world wars. I had never met a naval officer. No-one had suggested it might be a good career. At my grammer school I shrugged off the school's enthusiastic efforts to recruit me into the Combined Cadet Force. The nearest I came to anything remotely martial had been as a Baden-Powell cub. Proud though I was of the proficiency badge sewn on my uniform sleeve for cooking porridge over a camp fire, I didn't morph into a full-blown scout.

However, when I was thirteen a friend of the family took me with him for a holiday in Torquay. One day we went by steam train to Kingswear on the River Dart. We didn't catch the railway ferry across the river to Dartmouth. Instead we hired a rowing boat.

It was a perfect summer's day. We sat in the boat in the middle of the river, our oars holding our position in the turning of the tide, and drank in the peaceful scene. The sides of the valley rose steeply from the water's edge and the houses on the Dartmouth bank stacked one above the other before giving way to trees and fields and the sky.

At the upriver end of the town I saw that hill for the first time. It was largely covered in well maintained parkland but at the top sat the College. It was an impressive sight. Built of red brick and white stone it was surrounded by stone ramparts, from the middle of which rose a tall flag pole with a white ensign at its top, lifting in the breeze. At first sight it seemed strangely out of place, yet it didn't entirely dominate the town or the hill. It was so well sited, far enough apart from the town, sufficiently in tune with the hill itself, that it seemed more a fitting crown set comfortably on its head.

But it was the river itself that seduced me, whispering and singing to me as it flowed from the north, the trees on its banks reaching down into the water as if drinking. Then, as it passed beneath us, it beckoned me to follow its broadening passage between the two castles, standing guard, one on each rocky side of its mouth, and into a sun-sparkling and ever expanding sea.

Sitting here I felt safe and at home in the valley's embrace, safe enough for the soul to yield to the faintly murmured promises of the sea and the river's come-with-me caresses, willing me to follow her into it. She aroused my fertile imagination, well primed as it was by books I'd read of maritime derring-do (among which, ironically, was Arthur Ransome's "We Didn't Mean to go to Sea") with her own tales of her turbulent history … the 164 ships gathering in the deep-water harbour to set off for the second crusade… the attack by a thousand-strong army of Bretons, repulsed around the corner at Blackpool Sands…Walter Raleigh bringing back into harbour his pirated Spanish treasure ships…Humphrey Gilbert colonising Newfoundland and the fishing fleets following his lead to new found fishing grounds…the Spanish Armada…the Pilgrim Fathers…

the 480 allied ships gathered in the river for the D-day invasion…

So it was that the whole experience of sitting in that boat at the turning of the tide sank into a deep pool of the unconscious and quietly went to sleep.

Indeed, even as late as the summer of 1953, strolling with a lock-keeper's daughter along the bank of Hamburg's River Alter, I was reading a speech aloud to her from "Hamlet," in German. "Sein oder nichtsein, das ist hier die Frage…" Poor girl! Not a hint of a sea-faring future troubled my romantic adolescent brain. Sixth Form and 'A' Levels in English and German remained an unquestioned certainty.

Then in the autumn, seemingly without warning, a light switched on.

In quick succession I wrote to the Admiralty for information and discovered that entry was for the first time no longer confined to public school boys; grammar school boys would be considered. I signed up for their entrance examination, arranged myself extra maths lessons at school to get up to speed with the standard required, sat and passed the exams in May 1954 and, after a three-day residential interview, was accepted as a cadet. So there I was, marching up the hill in September 1954.

The thing is, I didn't consciously know or think it at the time but it was just what I needed: to get right away from a confined and fractious family life and other people's expectations. To go my own way. It's as if the mini-universe of little stars inside me came of their own accord into alignment and I just did it. And it catapulted me into a completely different way of life and social milieu, a multiplicity of new challenges through which I experienced and learned so many things I may well not otherwise have known; for all of which I am deeply thankful.

So here I was again in 1961, sitting alone in a rowing boat in the middle of the river, holding it steady against the turning of the tide, feeling the peace of it, the stillness before action, all options again open, choices to be made, upriver or down, the barely heard whisper of my own river history now an infinitesimal part of the river's song. And on that happy if melodramatic note, I leant back on the oars and pulled firmly to the river's bank and another life.

I eventually got the 'A' Levels anyway and went to university – but in my own way and in my own time. Cue for Frank Sinatra singing "I did it my way!"

No Turning Back

Sitting on his throne on the beach
Canute knew
not simply that he couldn't
stop
the incoming tide
but that he
and we
could have no influence whatsoever

on the ebb
and flow
of the sea
and that
with each visit it made
the beach
would never be

the same again.

LOW TIDE

Here we go again! The moon! She's a hard mistress! Never mind the pain, she is unrelenting. So again, the tide is turning. I can feel the sea pulling through me, little by little, my life-blood leaching, leaving me high and drying, heavy with loss.

Leaving me again with the painful awareness of my naked state. With a skin too sensitive to the toxic touch of so many pieces of plastic left scattered across my body. Tangles of fish-netting. Strands of nylon rope. Empty seashells, sad markers of fellow lives lost.

And now there will be dogs. Digging with their claw feet and crapping. Sea-edge beaks piercing and pulling out my living worms. Plastic forks, cigarette stubs, broken bottles, crushed beercans. Even the after-taste of sewage, as the sun dismisses my hope of rain and extracts the last of my bodily fluids.

Sometimes I think I'll not be able to bear it again. But I do.

And sometimes I find relief.

Someone finds delight in a little rock pool left behind. That gives me pleasure and reminds me it won't be long before the sea will claim me back again.
And a lady walks along my sealine picking up the plastic

pieces. The birds whisper that she turns them into images of the sea.

Best of all, I have noticed with pleasure that each high tide has been growing a little higher and I have hopes that sometime soon I shall be forever immersed and alive with a living sea.

Plastic ship upon a plastic ocean by Elaine Powley

A Deep Rumble in Rabaul

Susie drove us up to the edge of a moonscape of ash and pumice. An old man carrying a long, heavy knife stopped us. Ahead was an elaborate pattern of markers made from old branches that defined a 'road' and barred all other approaches across the ash. He was the 'gate-keeper'. And he charged admittance to anyone wishing to view the volcano from 'his' domain. A wonderful bit of free enterprise, wresting a living out of disaster.

No-one seemed to challenge his right to do it. In fact, Susie not only assured him she'd pay him later, she invited him to come with us and to tell us the story of the eruptions. Which he did with gusto. Furthermore, she had some time ago advised him on customer relations. She discovered that he would greet tourists by waving his arms at them vigorously to get them to stop. However, his hand was still attached to his knife. Much alarmed, they would promptly turn back, sure he was about to attack them. But he'd been quite unconscious of his knife and couldn't fathom why everyone ran away, because all locals carry such knives for their work, like extensions of their arms. Now his knife is far less on show.

Susie was of Scottish descent but born in Rabaul. Her husband was an Australian. It was her father who constructed several of the original buildings, including the bank, a cement works and the Rabaul Hotel, which Susie ran and was her home.

Rabaul's harbour is spectacular, the wharf central to what was once a pretty town of traditional and colonial buildings, a park and smart hotels. It was originally laid out and built on a spacious grid plan by Germans, so that the main streets were wide boulevards, with palm trees and shrubs down the middle.

But in and around the harbour are four volcanoes. Vulcan,

Tavurvur, The Mother and The Daughter. Vulcan appeared as an island out of nowehere in an eruption in 1878 and was immediately planted with coconuts. Then in 1937 Vulcan and Tavurvur erupted together, from which Vulcan emerged as a huge mountain. In 1994 they repeated their

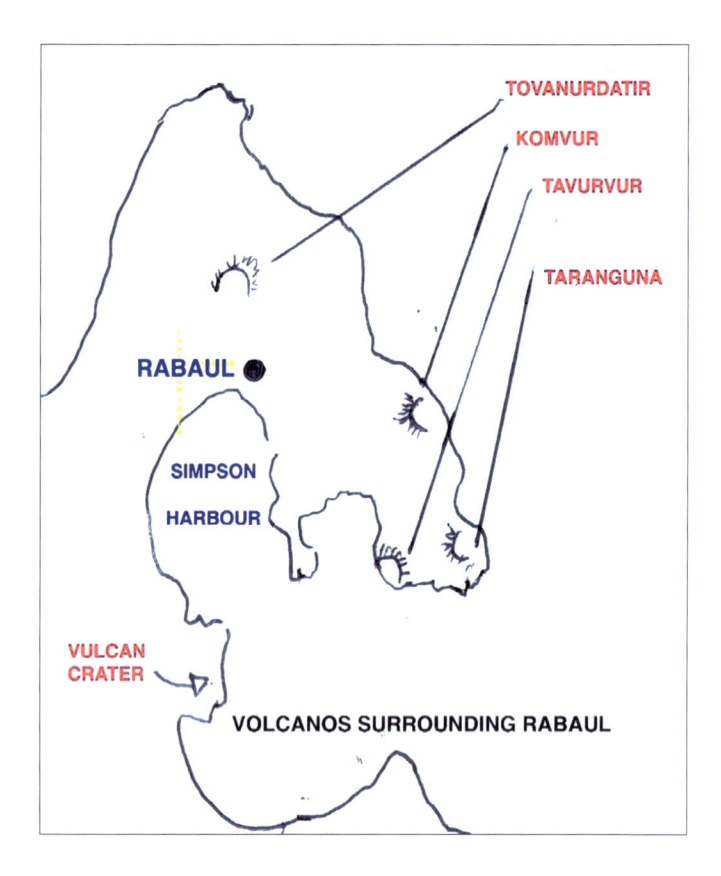

VOLCANOS SURROUNDING RABAUL

double act and destroyed half the city. The rest was badly damaged by looting. By the time we arrived only some of the lovely houses were still lived in and well maintained. The rest were dilapidated or taken over by squatters.

The destruction was not caused by lava. Buildings collapsed under the sheer weight of ash and pumice. Susie and her husband worked day and night to save their hotel, clearing ash and pumice from the roof and fending off looters. Her father's bank was not so lucky. It is now part of the moonscape. However, the vault had been built so strong that looters failed to reach the thousands of banknotes stored within.

Two weeks before our ship docked alongside the wharf, Tavurvur woke up again in a series of explosions spewing ash columns over seven kilometres high and red gouts of lava into the sea.

A Vulcanology Observatory stands on the ridge above the harbour, commanding a view of all four volcanoes. One of its functions is to provide early warning of volcanic activity. There was no warning given two weeks ago. The telephones at the Observatory had been cut off the week before because the government department funding the operation had neglected to pay the bill.

"I just couldn't face going through all that again," Susie confessed. "Enough is enough. I bundled my daughter and a few clothes into the car and drove. But I couldn't see where I was going through the smoke and thought, no! This is crazy. I can't leave now."

So she stayed to fight off the ash again.

The volcano was still smoking when we arrived. The old man led us to the water's edge. Two young boys were boiling eggs in it. Suddenly the volcano rumbled and with a loud bang belched forth a huge, angry coil of ash and smoke, high into the sky. Boulders arced upwards through it and fell sizzling into the sea. Someone shouted, "Run! run!" And we ran.

The Last Dance

In a swish and swirl
of tafetta dresses
lovely princesses
twirl in the arms
of other men
while I sink in my chair
on the brink of despair
wondering when I'll be able
to hold her again.

The touch of her fingers
still lingers on my skin
leaving me yearning
burning to tell her -
but where oh where to begin?!
so here I am turning
to drink again.

Even now as she
and her partner pass
I can only push my nose
deeper into my glass.

Oh, I know this is perverse
a crippling curse
I know I need to fight
this infection
this fear of rejection.

Now from behind me
a soft voice whispers in my ear
words that threaten to blind me
with joyful tears of relief
words I so badly wished to hear
banishing every iota of grief.

So let's take the chance, she says,
to join in with the last dance,
leading me onto the floor
where she tells of undressing
and caressing and of
leading me gladly to bed
and more, lots more

Enough said!!

The Race

February 1959 in Hobart, Tasmania

"Shall I do your back, sir?"

"Yes, please, Woods. And I'll do yours."

Alan shut his eyes and to his surprise felt his body sigh and settle as Woods slapped and spread the grease over his back with his big hands. Then, as he greased Woods in turn and felt how broad and strong his back was and yet how soft its surface felt to his touch, he marvelled at how circumstances could so shift the formality of command on board their ship into such intimacy.

Yet here they were now, doing their duty, along with four more of their crew, sitting in a small boat in their swimming trunks, fully greased. Alan could feel his back already cooking in the sun as sweat battled its way out. But they had been warned. The water they were about to enter was very cold.

"How cold must it be," he wondered, "to warrant this much grease?"

"Very, very," said Woods, resigned to his lot. "Better than nothing, I suppose." Alan shivered in spite of the sun.

And then there were the sharks. They had been spotted in the river that morning. So for their protection the swimmers had been given little bags of shark repellent to tie to their trunks. He wondered what on earth the active ingredient could be in so small a bag.

"Must be powerful stuff, Woods! Do you think the sharks'll be impressed?"

"More likely addicted, sir!"

Their boat was at the end of a line of similar boats tied to buoys just a few metres apart along one side of the River Derwent's wide estuary, each with men in trunks waiting for the start of the annual race to the other side.

Alan's ship was a British Royal Navy aircraft carrier tied alongside in Hobart's harbour. It was on an official visit to a number of Australian ports. Its crew of seventeen hundred had been invited to enter a team. The six lucky volunteers were the same men who had, rather embarrassingly, won practically all the races at an army gala they'd been invited to in Aden a few months ago. But that was in a swimming pool. Now they sat in silent contemplation of the water and its hidden depths – and the distance to the farther shore.

Meanwhile, the Mayor of Hobart, himself an ex-naval stoker, was on an official visit to Alan's ship. A block of a man in his sixties, formally dressed in a grey if rumpled suit and well-used, heavy black shoes, he puffed his way up to the bridge, well dined and wined, and boyishly delighted with revisiting the Navy all these years later as a dignitary. Through the Captain's binoculars he examined the waiting contestants.

"One of your boys going to win? "

The Captain laughed. "Perhaps. If any of them do, it'll be one of those two you see in the bows. The big fellow – Woods – is a champion swimmer. He should do quite well."

The Mayor studied Alan and Woods. "Right. I'll keep an eye on them." He laughed. "You may not think it, looking at me now, but years ago when I first came here, I swam this race!" He shook his head wryly. "Came nowhere near winning, though."

A fog-horn echoed across the estuary, the signal for entering the water, ready for the start. "Jesus!" exclaimed Woods. "More grease!" shouted one of the others.

Another blast on the horn and the race began. "Good luck, lads," said the Mayor.

August 1898 in Mahrisch-Ostrau, Silesia

Alan's grandfather, Hermann, hadn't been feeling very well for a couple of days but here he was, in his swimming costume and sitting in a boat on the River Oder, waiting for the race to begin. More competitors sat waiting in other boats. With him were three of his club mates and their trainer, who had worked them all hard for weeks for this annual five kilometre race. But Hermann was the favourite to win.

The first whistle pierced the air. Time to dive in and line up ready for the start. He waited until the others had entered the water, then his trainer slapped him on the back.

"Just swim as you have for the last couple of weeks, my boy, and you'll win. Go well!"

Hermann stood up, positioned himself astern as the trainer balanced the boat in the bow, and dived. But as he hit the water his body exploded with pain. It knocked the breath out of him. As he recovered his wits and manoeuvred himself into position, he realised he couldn't feel his legs. When the starting whistle blew he wasn't sure if he could move them. But he started to swim.

He couldn't understand what was happening to him. He couldn't tell if his legs were moving or not. It was clear though that he was falling behind the other swimmers.

"This is crazy," he thought."I'll have to stop."

But as he came to the first bridge he could see the spectators leaning over its wall and cheering them on.

He heard a voice shouting, "Come on, Hermann! Get a move on! What's the matter with you?!"

He swam on, under the bridge.

"The next bridge," he thought. "The next bridge. I'll get out at the next bridge."

His trainer, realising something was very wrong, rowed after him. "Hermann!" he shouted, holding out his hand to him." You should get out now!"

But he refused and swam on, powered only by his strong arms and shoulders and his pride but falling ever further behind. And each time he reached a bridge and saw the spectators he said to himself, "the next bridge. The next bridge."

Thus he reached the finishing line, last by a long way. Quite a crowd, among them his mother, was waiting for him as he was dragged out of the water. He tried standing up but collapsed, unable to move.

1959 in Hobart

Both Woods and Alan set off at a steady pace, aware of the distance they had to cover, but were soon ahead of the rest of their team and were keeping up with the local swimmers. Alan was a bit bothered at first that he couldn't actually see the other swimmers, or the other side of the river, but his mind and body soon yielded to the relaxed repetition of each stroke of his arms and the intimate feel and flow of the water. Until something slid along one of his legs. His whole body momentarily jerked to one side. Sharks! Bloody sharks!

"Oh, come off it, you idiot," he thought, as he re-established his rhythm."Bloody weed! – I hope."

Back on the ship's bridge,"What's your chap doing?" said the mayor. "He's wandering off course…caught in a cross-current, perhaps…" He laughed. "It's taking him round in a circle. Well, lad…that's the end of your race."

The only hazards Alan was aware of were more bits of weed. Each time they touched him his body jerked. Phantom bloody sharks! He laughed inwardly at the power of his imagination. But why were his legs feeling numb. Was it so cold?

"That's good," said the Mayor. "One of the safety boats

has caught up with him." "Good," said the Captain. "I see Woods is up with the leaders."

"He's refusing to get into the boat...." said the Mayor. "He's just following it to the finish. Well, good for you, lad..."

At last he reached the other side of the river and stumbled ashore. He was tired and his legs were wobbly. Most of the spectators had left but someone called out "Good onya mate!!" He waved his thanks and climbed back into the safety-boat and was returned to his ship. The next day the Captain requested his presence on the bridge.

"The Mayor of Hobart," he said, "was so impressed with your effort in yesterday's race that he wanted to award you this special cash prize..." he handed Alan an envelope, "…for doggedness." He smiled. "Congratulations!"

1898 in Mahrisch – Ostrau

They presented Hermann with a certificate for finishing the race, which his mother accepted on his behalf. And for the next year she worked tirelessly, pushing her son harder than his trainer ever had, until he was able to walk again – though not swim and certainly not run.

Dilemma

"You must go," she says. "You know you must."

I am sitting by her bed holding her hand and trying not to cry.

" I can't possibly! Not now. Not until you're better."

"Darling, I am dying." Her hand tightens in mine. " The longer you stay, the more likely you'll die with me. So. You have to go. You know it's true."

"But Mutti–!"

"But nothing!" She sighs and shuts her eyes with a grimace of pain.

"Listen, my darling, I have always loved you as if you were my own daughter – you know that, don't you? "

I nod and squeeze her hand.

"And I have always made sure you and your brother have had a safe and welcoming home to come back to."

"Yes, yes, you have. I know. And love you for it." I kiss her hand and hold it to my cheek.

It is true. She always was the still centre of our lives. However many towns or countries we lived in, home remained the same, in her image. And when eventually we settled in one place and my brother and I could make proper friends without worrying about having to leave them, she welcomed them in and charmed them with her gentle attention and famous pastries. She was, they declared, the best pastry cook in the city. No! In the whole of Europe!

I find myself smiling, though on the brink of tears.

"What?" she says. "What is it?"

"Pastries!" I say and laugh. For a moment her pain disappears in the pleasure of my remembering and I kiss her hand again.

And I'm thinking, yes, even when my father was so rarely at home, travelling to China or Italy or England on business, she managed to keep his presence alive so strongly in the home that we half expected to find him drinking coffee in his study.

Now he is actually here, in the flesh, though he's out at the moment, shopping of all things. He'll probably bring back a little treat of some sort. A favourite chocolate, perhaps. Though she'll probably give it to me to eat, then tell him how nice it was.

"But this home," she says, "is no longer a safe place. Even if

I were well, I couldn't make it safe. Your father can't. Your friends can't. No-one can."

I can see how the effort hurts her. My eyes close. Her pain is sucking all the words out of me.

"What do they tell you to do? Your friends?"

"To leave," I mutter.

"Of course they do."

Her eyes close slowly as her head sinks back into the pillow. They stay shut so long I wonder if she's fallen asleep. I hope so.

But no, she hasn't. Eyes still shut, she says, "Thank god your brother had the sense not to come back. He'll be safe in Canada."

She opens her eyes and looks at me with a sudden intensity.

"You could easily go to England. There's still time. You speak good English. Your auntie Olga has already offered to take you in...." she smiles "...and you can feast on her famous poppyseed cake!"

"Yes." I shake my head and laugh in spite of myself. "That's true."

She's not going to give up. What can I say? "But the point is…" She waits for me to finish but I can't.

She says it for me. "Your father is staying."

"Yes."

"So you think you also should stay."

She is not asking me, she is telling me.

"Yes, yes, I do, I do – don't you see? I must."

"Why?"

This is so unlike her. Not unkind, exactly, but...hard... unyielding.

"Because..."

"He needs you."

That hurts. I feel myself flinching. The weary way she says it. An accusation, almost, a challenge. Almost as if she thinks it couldn't be true and I'm stupid to think so. I feel myself bridling.

"Yes!" I shake my head, telling myself to calm down.

"Yes," I say, more measured now, "He does. He really does."

She says nothing. Just looks at me. I see the pain in her eyes.

"No," she says at last. "He really doesn't."

I stare at her, shocked.

"Listen to me now. Your father loves us both in his own way and he'll accept our help when he feels he needs it but, in the end, he doesn't really need either of us. Or anyone."

I begin to object but she stops me – "Please ! – Just listen. He is the most independent person I have ever known, and the most proud and obstinate. He'll be damned if he'll let some petty official tell him what he can or can't do or threaten him and his family. That's why he is still here. It's not all about love. And, as you well know, he's a gambler. Not just cards and horses but business, people, religion, politics – whatever else. He wins, he loses, but either way it doesn't bother him. He laughs, turns himself round and carries on as if nothing has happened. He's fearless. Either way he still comes home bearing gifts with a theatrical flourish and a joke. Charming as ever. Don't you agree?"

Oh my dear father! Yes I do.

"And we two – we love him for it, don't we? In fact we both adore him. Colourful. Larger than life. But! – my dear – you mustn't let that bind you to him or spend your life trying to make him love you more than he is able to. Not just for your sake but for his. You see, it's his life he is gambling with now. How do you think he keeps this roof over our heads and food on the table? By continuing to run a successful business. And how does he do that? By hoodwinking or bribing the officials he needs approval from. And that's the least of it."

With a little snort of laughter she adds, "He's even gambling that I'll die before it's too late for him to go. "

She sinks back onto the pillow, exhausted. I'm trembling. My inner world is melting away.

"So, my darling. He loves you and won't tell you to leave. But it will be better for both of you if you do. You'll be safe and he'll have one less problem to solve. And he won't tell you to stay–"

She pauses and takes a deep breath. "Will you go? Please."

I can't hold back my tears any longer. "Oh Mutti, I'm so sorry!"

I'm struggling for breath and to stop my body shaking. She watches me with sad eyes and waits. At last I can speak.

"Yes, Mutti. I'll go."

Then nightly sings the staring owl, Tu-Who

For my grand-daughter

I wonder if you have ever seen an owl – or heard it sing?

There are many different kinds of owl. For example, there's the long-eared owl, called that because, for an owl, its ears are long. Though compared to a horse's ears they are very short. And hardly worth calling ears at all if you put them next to an elephant's ears.

Then there's the short-eared owl, called that because it has short ears. In fact, they are so short you can't actually see them – unless the owl is cross. Then they appear as little tufts on either side of the head at the top, which is meant to frighten off whoever is bothering them. I doubt that it would frighten off an elephant.

Actually, what looks like tufty ears aren't really ears at all. Real owl ears, whether they have tufts or not, are just slits, one on each side of the head. But they are very good for hearing with. They know exactly where their food is by listening to its slightest movement.

As far as I know, we haven't any short or long-eared owls at

Lund Head. But we do have tawny owls. And why are they called that ….? Yes….they are tawny – which is a shorter way of saying the colour of their feathers is a yellowish brown. I saw one once, as I drove our car one evening into our entrance road through the field. At first I saw a lot of rabbits. They always come out of their burrows in the evening. But I noticed one in particular, sitting hunched up by the roadside. Or was it something pretending to be a rabbit?

I stopped to have a closer look. I thought, "That can't be a rabbit. It has no rabbity ears – or tail."

Then it turned its head and looked straight at me with round staring eyes. It looked very cross.

 "Of course I'm not a rabbit ! "it seemed to say. "I'm an owl. A tawny owl, what's more. Use your eyes, silly grandpa". And it turned away in disgust and flew off.

I haven't seen a tawny owl since then but we do hear them at night, especially in winter. They are the ones that sing "tu-whit tu-who."

Barn owls, on the other hand, we hear and see a lot of. They are called that because they often live in barns. Well, they do if they can find one. Farmers used to like having an owl living on the farm because it would help with catching mice. As you know, mice love to eat what the farmers grow, like wheat or turnips.

And owls like eating mice.

Some farmers used to build their barns with special doorholes high in the end wall to invite barn owls in – an invitation the owls were happy to accept – especially in England, where it rains a lot – for in the barn they can be out of the rain. Lots of stone-built barns have narrow windows in their walls – with no glass, of course – specially made to let air in but to keep the rain out. Owls could and still do use them as a way in. And that's why they are sometimes called 'owl slits'. As you know we have a big barn with owl slits. But, alas, no owl to squeeze through them.

But we often see barn owls flying across our garden. Usually they come as the daylight fades to night, gliding silently on their broad white wings, like ghosts in the dark, listening for their food. Which is why they are sometimes called 'ghost owls'.

Once I was standing under a very big fir tree in our garden when suddenly a huge barn owl leapt off a branch just above me and flew out so close to me I felt its wing tip brush my face. Luckily it wasn't singing at the time. For a barn owl doesn't merrily sing 'tu-whit tu-who'. It screeches, long and loud. And if your ear is too close it'll probably waggle so much with fright it'll fall off your head. You have been warned. And that's why it's sometimes called a 'screech owl'.

Would you like to know how many more names the Barn Owl has?

Well, here are some of them: white owl, silver owl, demon

owl, death owl, night owl, rat owl, church owl, cave owl, stone owl, monkey-faced owl, hissing owl, hobgoblin or hobby owl, dobby owl, white-breasted owl, golden owl, scritch owl, straw owl, barnyard owl, and delicate owl.

How about that ?! And you and I, we've only got three names each.

So now it's time to sing a quiet 'tu-whit tu-who and goodnight to you'.

Out of the darkness...?

Don't even think about it!

It's comfortable here, feather-wrapped
in the gentle darkness of sleeping.
Safely curled in my own dream-world.

Stop shaking my shoulder.
Stop!

For pity's sake.

Out of the darkness?
Why?
Into what?

The light?

No thanks. Done that.
T-shirt torn to tatters.
Eyes scorched with weeping.

Too terrible to watch
all the earth's bright colours leaching
into the hard-edged, stark
unequivocal DARK.

The Riddle on the Griddle

I stared at it intently. It sat smugly on the hearth, next to the wood stove. It would not tell me it's name. Would not! A few precious moments of my life died as I fought with it.

"Tell me. For goodness sake, tell me!" I said.

"Name? What name?" it replied.

"Your name, you wretch. I want it!"

"Your problem, mate," it said, "not mine. I don't need a name."

With furrowed brow, I ferreted through the labyrinth in search of the word.

The cat on the sofa awoke, stretched and yawned.

She stared at me intently.

"The rattling of your brains," she said, "woke me. Why don't you relax? Forget about whatever it is and look at me."

She stretched again, mewed winsomely and blinked.

"Why be bothered with such trivia when you could stroke me?"

I turned with a smile to the thingamajig on the hearth and said, "Yes, well, never mind, as long as I know what you're for, your name doesn't really matter, does it – for now."

"And while you're at it," the thingamajig said, "you haven't actually used me for months."

"True," I replied. "I'll just go and make some tea," I said.

Whereupon I lifted the thingamajig up by one of it's three little legs and placed it on the stove-top griddle.

"There," I said. "You stay there and soon you'll have a nice pot of tea sitting on you."

"That's more like it," it said.

"Then," I said to the cat, "you can sit on my lap and be stroked."

"It's the only way to go," she replied.

An apple a day

An apple fell
in front of his car

he stopped

and again
heard her voice

heard himself
wheedling
she needling
himself insisting
she resisting

as he pushed her to the ground

rubbed her face
in his dirt…

The fact is
he was the stronger

The fact is
he forced her to do it

The fact is
he made her pick it

he pushed it in her face
and made her bite

Much later they
fell exhausted
and slept….

shaken
he drove forward
to crush it
but
stopped

stepped
out of the car
held the apple
gently to his cheek
and wept.

Broken

He sat on a layer of dead leaves, his back slumped against a rock and his legs stretched out before him. His clothes were mud splashed and tattered, hardly recognisable as the fine-cut and flowing cloak and robe they once were. A tangled beard hid most of his face and straggled across his chest and in which insects and a family of mice had made their homes. He was asleep, though, and as time twitched its way through his body, his lips mumbled and muttered fragments of pages past, his fingers dancing arthritically to barely imagined little bursts of inner music. He was, in fact, stuttering his way to death.

And his progress was being watched closely by an owl, perched on the bottom branch of a nearby dead tree, and by a cat, sitting upright and alert at his feet.

"Any minute now," said the owl. "You'd better move further away, don't you think? It may be a bit explosive."

"As usual," said the cat, stretching her back.

"But for the last time," added the owl.

"We hope," added the cat.

At which the man's body stirred and stretched and moaned and lifted itself creakingly to its feet. And opened its eyes, recognised itself as a man and bellowed, "Where is my staff? Where is my great staff of ash?!!" He paused, took a deep breath and cried out, "Come to me, my ash, my lovely ash of power!"

For a moment it seemed the Earth stopped breathing. Then there was a rustling sound amongst the dead trees.

"Behind you!!" called the owl to the cat, who scurried out of the way to the top of a tree.

With which in a blaze of light the staff rose up from the forest floor and flew straight as an arrow towards the man, straight past his shaking hands and into the rock behind him with a crack of thunder – and split it into two. And knocked him to the ground.

"Oh, Athena save us! He's out of control!" hooted the owl as she flew down to perch on his shoulder.

The cat followed her from her tree and rubbed herself, purring, against his leg and licked his hand. "By Bastet!" she said, "Calm down now."

"That was unfortunate," the owl whispered in his ear. "Now then, can you remember what we agreed must be done?"

He seemed confused, so she started again. "What are you?" she asked. "A bird? Or a tiger? Or an elephant perhaps?"

"No, no," he shook his head and thought about it a long

time before muttering, apologetically, "A human being… a human."

"And can you remember what's special about you as a human?" asked the cat, who had now curled herself up in his lap.

"Yes," he sighed, as a tear hung on the brink of his lash. "I'm the last one in the whole world…and…I'm dying," he said.

"Yes," said the owl and cat together.

"And," said the human, struggling to his feet, while lifting the cat from his lap, "I made a promise."

"Yes," said the cat.

"You did," said the owl. "And now is the time to keep it."

The last human in the world stood as firmly as he could with his feet astride, took hold of his great ash staff of power with hands as far apart and as comfortably as possible, turned to face the largest remaining piece of rock, raised the ash pole above his head and with a roar that would startle a pride of lions brought down the staff at its middle point with his full weight and split the mighty staff in two.

Then he turned to face the cat and the owl and thrust each half of the staff into the soil on either side of his feet.

Whereupon, each half sprouted branchlets and leaves and began to grow into trees, while mini ash trees sprouted one after the other in the scorched earth all about them and as far as the eye could see through the dead forest.

The owl and the cat sang their delight.

"Better late than never," said the owl.

The cat purred her agreement.

And then they became aware the human had vanished into thin air and that a family of mice was scuttling past them into the newly sprouted wood.

Instead they were greeted by a wolf shaking his whole body as if he'd scrambled out of a river.

"By Artemis!" he exclaimed. "Save me from ever being a human again!"

THE THING IS...

Haiku variations

1.
The thing is I'll
hide in your shadow, your
sweet "thing" on the side

2.
Yet again you say
"the thing is…" and the sting is
I'm nothing to you.

3.
The thing is, my friend
nothing comes of nothing, so
please give me something.

4.
What is the thing?….just
watch it jump out of the hat!
Da,da!!! Hello THING!!!

5.
**SO LET THE BELLS RING
AND TOGETHER LET US SING
GLORY TO OUR THING.**

That's it then

It was one of those soft leather hold-everything handbags. Her hand dipped into it and searched for her purse, even before the other hand had finished shutting the fridge door. As ever she felt a little burst of irritation that it wouldn't swing shut on its own anymore. Always an extra push. Oh well. Not for much longer. Meanwhile the hand in the bag couldn't find the purse.

What the hell? Her mind and both hands suddenly focussed. Surely it was too big to be hidden. She froze. Oh Jesus! Panic slapped her in the face. Oh please no! She grabbed at the bag and turned it upside down, scattering its contents across the kitchen table. No purse. She searched again inside the bag. Empty.

Suddenly drained of energy she sank into a chair. The breath left her in a long sigh, almost a whimper. A moment of dazed silence.

Shit! All right. Think! When did I last see it? At the supermarket. Yes. I'd slipped the loop over my wrist after paying and, yes, I was still carrying it in my right hand, with the handbag hanging from my right shoulder and the shopping bag in the other hand. Then across the carpark to the… The car!

She ran into the garage and searched, her hands trembling,

aware he might come home at any minute. Nothing. Think. Not in the car. So… Come on! Before getting into the car. What did I do? I usually drop the purse into my handbag and then drop the handbag onto the passenger seat. Yes that's what I did. Thought I did. As usual. But…. what if the purse just fell on the floor and I didn't notice. She grimaced. In too much of a hurry. Maybe it's still in the carpark.

Telephone. She got up and stopped. They'll be closed, of course. She looked at her watch. Jesus! Nearly midnight. Go there now? Look for it? Goddammit! No! He'll be here soon. Have to leave it 'til the morning. Please,please, please! She looked at her watch again. Got to go to bed. Be asleep before he comes back.

In her bedroom she quickly undressed, found the bottle of sleeping tablets in the drawer under the bedside table, placed a couple of tablets on the table top along with the open bottle and lid. Glass of water! Mustn't forget the water. She stopped and surveyed the scene, took a deep breath, exhaled slowly and nodded. And now, she sighed with a sad self-mocking smile, sweet wind-battered bird, to bed. She manouevered herself under the duvet and switched off the light.

But she didn't sleep. Half an hour later she heard his car turn into the drive. His key in the door. A curse when the door stuck. Bloody door! His feet heavy on the wooden floor. Another door swung shut. Nothing discreet or delicate about his entrances! Moving about in the kitchen. The fridge door – that bloody fridge! Silence. Then footsteps approached. She sighed. She shut her eyes, rolled over on her side and started to breath with her mouth partly open, the air rasping a little as it passed her tongue and lips.

Her door opened abruptly. He stopped. He seemed to be gathering himself.

"Well, I'm home!" he announced, though not as loudly as she expected. She could smell the whiskey already. Noted the slurr in his diction. Said nothing, of course, but felt herself flinch. He stepped with exaggerated care across the room towards her. She forced her body to stay limp. He leant forward and touched her shoulder. She stirred a little in response, mumbled a few incoherent words, swallowed, turned back on her side and resettled into apparent oblivion.

"Asleep again are you?" Silence. "Oh, of course!" He sighed. "The pills. Shit."

A long silence. She was acutely aware of him standing next to the bed just looking at her. What was he doing? Oh my god, he's crying. Then suddenly he blew his nose and muttered, more to himself than to her: "that's it then." He sighed again. "That's bloody it." He turned, left the room, making a show of closing the door quietly behind him.

Suddenly she felt extraordinarily remote. That is indeed bloody it. But she knew it wouldn't be for him. He'd be back.

By seven thirty in the morning he had left for work grabbing one of the croissants she had bought. Then she got up. She'd hardly slept at all. Too wired up. But she had a shower, dressed, made sure her carry-on case was locked, ate the remaining croissant and called for a taxi.

"Take me to the supermarket first", she said. "The Lidl by the church. Then wait and take me to the station. OK?"

At the supermarket, heart in mouth, she asked about her purse. Soft red leather, about 9 inches long with zips and lots of pockets. Yes, indeed, they had such a purse. The trolley man found it in the carpark late last night.

She nearly collapsed with relief. Her hands trembled as she zipped it open, checking her cards – yes – her airline ticket – oh thank god ! – passport – yes – disposable mobile. Good.

"I think you'll find everything's there," said the cashier. "He's an honest man, is Tom."

"Yes, yes, of course. I'm sorry. But you won't believe how worried I've been. My whole life is in this purse." The cashier smiled and nodded. "Here's Tom now."

She ran over to him as he came through the door. Nearly bumped into him. "Tom," she said, "I'd like to thank you for finding my purse last night. So -" she hesitated and smiled, nodding – "thank you. Thank you so so much." She shook his hand vigorously, leaned towards him and, much to his surprise, gave him a kiss on the cheek.

"That's all right, ma'am," he managed to say. She continued nodding to Tom and the cashier, then turned abruptly and returned to the taxi, waving.

"Thanks for waiting." She settled into her seat. After a minute or two she leaned forward. "Actually, can you drop me this side of the bridge. I'd just like to walk across the bridge to have a last look at the river before catching my train."

When she was half way across the bridge she stopped and leant on the balustrade to watch the river pass beneath. Its gentle progress calmed her. She smiled and opened her purse and took out her mobile, prodded a number and waited, still smiling. A voice responded.

"Oh my dear, dear Babs, I can't tell you how good it is to hear your voice! " She laughed at the reply. "I'm half way across the bridge and will be with you in a few minutes. Will you wait for me, my darling?" she added, pretending doubt, and laughed again at the reply. "See you very soon!"

She turned once more to the river, leaned over the balustrade, dropped the phone into the water below. "That's finally it." Then she strode towards the station, pulling her little carry-on case behind her.

Indecision

How well I remember
the joy of leaping
endlessly
without hesitation
from rock to rock along the shore

so fleet of foot,
the body so sure
of size, shape and distance

so unaware of the dark
that lurked longingly
beneath and between,
I laughed at my burgeoning shadow
on the cliff face

hands and feet together
hauled me upwards
from ledge to ledge
in pursuit of her sun-tanned legs.

How difficult to forget
the seagull's screech
as its ice-polished eye
pinned my cheek to the weather-worn cliff,
pierced the brain
let the darkness in

all motion lost
limbs locked
no longer knew
what to do

suspended
above the approaching sea
time lingered mockingly

until at last
thought broke through
making notes
calculating
arguing
trying to decide

until at last

I placed a foot
found a handhold
heaved myself once more upward

just as her feet
flipped out of sight

over the top.

Then I knew
I had lost her.

An Invitation

Every night
there is a woman standing
at the edge of the sea
feet just in the water
savouring the grains of sand
as they cleanse her soles
watching the horizon
longing to accept
the moon's invitation
to swim down her silver path –

and watching her tonight
I think she might.

because many miles
beneath her feet
she connects
sole to sand-pricked sole
with a girl at the edge
of another sea though
in truth the same water
facing the morning sun
and its invitation to swim
down its golden path –

and seeing her this day
I think she may.

From Hamburg to Hull Hurricanes Hardly Happen…

As we leave the dock in Hamburg the radio warns us of gales at sea.

" Force 10 to hurricane force 12," it says. "Coming in from the south west, up the north German coast."

Just where we're about to go.

"Oh, they always say things like that," says the pilot, with a shrug.

Ironic, after three months at sea, storm-free, to be caught by a storm in what should be the last night of the voyage. Elaine and I joke about it. After all, it's true, isn't it, that from Hamburg to Hull hurricanes hardly happen? In fact, I don't mind. I'm quite looking forward to it.

At the Elbe's mouth the pilot leaves us with a wave of his hand. "So they were right for once!" he shouts through the wind. "Enjoy!"

Then the engines gear themselves up to meet a mighty sea. Wind force 11 already. Massive waves crash onto the bow. The whole ship judders and shudders with the impact, as heavy sheets of sea are flung bodily against the bridge windows, obliterating our view. But the good ship Tikeibank rides the waves well, ploughing up, down, up and through. With each heave, the mass of water sluices in all directions off the containers and vehicles and even a luxury ocean-going yacht wrapped in white polythene, all of them strapped firmly with cables and bolts to the deck. Firm enough to hold fast. While below in the holds plywood creaks and coconut and palm oil swing and slurp in their tanks. Speed of progress is down to 5 knots. Direction, an act of faith in radar and holding hard to the wheel. Luckily, our course is into the wind, else we'd have to heave to, which really would be uncomfortable.

Actually, I enjoy the exhilaration of riding a storm. The sight and sound of it. Moving with the ship's response to the pulse of the sea. The sense of being in tune with her, as a rider might be with a horse. And I have faith in this vessel, built as she was for all manner of seas and cargos. Yet even now I wonder at the ease with which we can feel so safe in the little enclosed world of a ship in bad weather at sea, or, on land in a tent, when in fact the elements have it in their power to destroy us utterly at any moment. That's how it is here and now. It doesn't occur to me that the vessel might fail – though another part of me really knows it might. But then we're inside the boat, not outside on deck, clinging to the rail, staggering into the wind, as those three men I see through the windows are.

And accidents sometimes do happen.

An exceptionally huge wave causes it. The rope-store covers on the foc'sle are letting in water. Four feet of it already in the store. The Chief Officer, the Bosun and the "Bear" are struggling up the deck in their yellow waterproofs, when the full force of the sea catches them as it breaks over the bow. The Chief falls awkwardly, smashing his knee against the hatch cover, as the bosun is flung against the guard-rail and gashes his forehead and as the "Bear", grabbing at him, wrenches a thumb. I watch as they struggle back. "For a terrible moment," the Chief says later, "I thought the bosun had been swept overboard."

In the well equipped ship's 'hospital', they are patched up temporarily. But the Chief needs surgery to his knee. It's badly swollen and probably smashed. For now he is sedated and kept in bed. He'll be all right until we arrive in Hull.

Elsewhere, we learn from the radio, in the same storm, a ship carrying fertilizer has lost her engines and is drifting towards a gas rig. A collision could be explosive. Ten men are being lifted off the rig but the ship's captain is determined to re-start his engines. He refuses to let his men go. His ship drifts closer to the rig. Then, with just 500 metres to spare, the engines leap into life; disaster is averted.

Eventually we fall into our beds, surfing as we sleep. We awake at anchor at Spurn Point, awaiting the tide to allow us passage up the Humber to the George V dock – and home.

But then! – the George V lock gate rams had failed and needed replacing. More waiting. "Oh dear," said the captain. It was clearly not good for the patient, who should really be in hospital.

Enter the RAF Air Sea Rescue in their yellow helicopter, the very same that rescued the gas men and five people off a yacht. Mission accomplished with impressive efficiency and good humour.

We waited for the pilot to take us home that evening. Ho, ho! We reached the Humber mouth only to be told the tugs wouldn't take us because of the 60 mph winds blowing at the dock. The pilot blasphemed and so – back to anchorage. Next morning? Well...

...we tried again. A cliffhanger. The problem this time, the tide. Complicated things are tides, which, as we know, waiteth for no man. It was a neap tide, when high tide is at its lowest. Even lower when the wind blows against it. Changing all the time, unpredictably. We'd not know until there, at the lock.

At last we were pointing directly into it. Men appeared on the moles, studying the plimsol line. Telephones rang. The captain earnestly beseeched the Lord above. "Sorry," he said, "but you can't come in. Too deep in the water." 35cm below the allowed draught. Too close to the bottom. So, back to anchor.

Everyone visibly slumped. So many people looking forward to the end of their voyage, with arrangements for going home made and broken, again. We felt the same. Bereft suddenly. Missing our children and the homecoming they will have gone out of their way to make special. We each coped with it in our own way. My wife out on deck with the sea and sky, the size of nature around her and later with a book of Melanesian art; me by talking it through with the captain and getting down to more writing, finding a way into the space I'd reserved for such an event, the fallback position. Our feelings ebbed and flowed during the day and we talked about it. Played Scrabble. Prayed for success the next day, Sunday – for the captain was determined to try again.

So, to Round Three. A lovely cold, sunny day. Good for messing about in boats. Reached the lock at about 1400. Nicely lined up. But! – no. Not enough clearance. Aborted again. Shit and damnation. Messing about is right!

Round Four on Monday. At last, at three in the morning, we crept through the lock to our final berth of the voyage in the King George Dock in Hull, much to the relief and delight of all the crew.

The King's Chair

Once upon a time there was a king who didn't like sitting on his throne. It was so uncomfortable.

But every morning he had to sit on it, as people in his kingdom gathered in the throne-room to ask him for advice or favours. Or to sort out quarrels. Or to decide how wrongdoers should be punished.

By lunchtime his bottom was sore and his back ached. So when everyone had left the room he was glad to stand up at last and have a good stretch.

One day, as his stretch had turned into a big yawn, in ran the little Princess, his granddaughter.

"Hello, Grandpa," she shouted.

He was so surprised, his crown nearly fell off. The little princess laughed to see it perched on the King's nose.

"It's lucky you've got a big nose, Grandpa!"

"It's what noses are for," he said. "And ears," he added.

He took off the crown and put it on her head – except that it went completely over her head and rested on her shoulders.

"And your nose and ears, little shrimp, are so small they can't hold the crown up at all. It's lucky you've got big-enough shoulders."

"I'm not a shrimp," she giggled from inside the crown. "I'm a Princess. Can I sit on the throne?"

"By all means, your Royal Highness." He bowed and retrieved his crown, then lifted her onto the throne, where she sat with a straight back and little legs dangling over the edge of the seat.

"You can sit on it as long as you like," he said. "I'd be happy not to sit on it ever again."

"Really, Grandpa?"

"Really," he sighed.

Both of them were quiet for a while. But the little Princess was thinking hard.

Then she asked, "What's your favourite chair, Grandpa?"

"Oh, that's easy," said the king. "My Royal Deckchair in my Private Garden." He smiled at the thought. "Preferably under the Royal Apple Tree," he added.

"Well, why don't you sit in your Royal Deckchair in your Private Garden under the Royal Apple Tree to see all those people?"

The King laughed. "What a lovely idea! But what if it were too cold or raining?"

"Oh, that's easy. You could move your Deck Chair into your study or the drawing room, in front of a nice log fire."

"But where would all the people wait? Can't have them all standing about in the garden or in my study, can I?"

"Well," said the little Princess, thinking hard. "I know.

They could all be in another room – like here, in the Throne Room – and come into the garden or study one or two at a time."

"But then I'd be sitting low down and they'd be standing up, looking down at me. Can't have that! The whole point of having a throne at the top of some steps is so they have to look up at me."

"Well..." She paused then laughed. "I know! they could sit on deck chairs as well, only theirs could be a bit smaller and plainer than yours, and your Royal Deck Chair could be really colourful and have padded arms, with a cushion for the head and a picture of a crown on top..."

"Ah," said the King. "Yes... but..."

But there was no stopping the little Princess now. Her mind was popping with ideas.

"And Grandma could knit you a blanket with lots of crowns and flowers all over it, so if it was a bit cold outside but not really cold enough to go indoors, you could wrap it round you ... and the others could have plain brown or green blankets...and everyone waiting in the throne room could have deck chairs to sit on as well so they wouldn't get fidgety or too tired with standing... and they could play skittles to pass the time, have competitions and...."

"And maybe they'd forget what they came for in the first place..." finished the King, laughing. "It's a lovely idea but I'm afraid it wouldn't work... you see..."

"But why ever not?" she said. "You are the King, aren't you?"

The king fell silent and looked at her for a long time, until she began wriggle. Then he laughed again.

"Yes," he said very firmly, "I am indeed the King."

And so, that is what happened – everything the little Princess had suggested. Some of his Council complained a bit at first but he was, after all, indeed the King.

When Grandma, the Queen, heard about it – especially the bit about her knitting – she said, "Well, I never! Whatever next?"

Well, for one thing, the Queen's knitting was so successful, she now runs a huge team of knitters whose work is exported all over the world. Not just Royal blankets, but things like Royal covers for eggs, mobile phones, coffee pots – even covers for tree trunks – or anything else you care to mention. They can cover it.

And for another thing, the King's Royal Skittle Team has won the World Skittle Competition Cup for three years running.

And the Little Princess? She is now a much respected member of the King's Royal Council.

Words Best Unspoken

Again I watch her gallop
standing in the stirrups
eyes hot with a future
without me.

I watch my words
like knives beaten in bitterness
fly again, slowly slowly,
across the space between us
and one by one
with easy precision
slip silently into her breast.

Again !
For god's sake
not again !
I watch her fall to the ground
so slowly, slowly
and hear her back
break.

Entertaining the Cows

My first experience of live theatre was, sad to say, traumatic. It was in the autumn of my last year at primary school. I was ten years old. Our teacher, Miss Hoare, announced that there would be a school play before Christmas and that our class would write and perform it. We all had to look for a story to adapt and bring our suggestions to class. I offered one from Arthur Ransome's "Old Peter's Russian Tales", a copy of which I dutifully presented to the teacher. To my surprise it was the one she chose. To my shock I was asked if I would adapt it.

I suppose it was a compliment. I was one of the bright boys, one of only seven in the class (of over 40) who later passed the eleven-plus exam for a place at grammar school. But what did I know about plays? We did no drama at school and neither saw nor read plays. And I didn't know how to say 'no'. It was more than that, of course. It didn't occur to me that I could say 'no'. Indeed, I was flattered. I was flushed with being chosen. Wanted to shine. At the same time I felt the weight of expectation, of responsibility and an increasing fear of failure. For some reason people kept assuming I could handle whatever they asked me to do. So there I was, suspended, as it were, in a little cloud, unable to move.

Miss Hoare thought it would help if I had a co-writer. She asked for a show of hands, which all, as ever, automatically rose in the air. I chose Ian Lambert. A mistake. As I found out very clearly one lunchtime in the playground. I was standing under a huge tree at the playground's edge, asking (begging?) Ian to help me and he simply shook his head and walked away. I hope that's not an overly melodramatic account of a writer's block.

In the end Miss Hoare put me out of my misery and wrote the play herself. I was given a small part to play in it. At the time I had a bamboo fipple flute which I could actually play and which I offered as a prop. The play opens with a boy sitting on a log in a wood playing his pipe. That was to be me. But he doesn't get very far into the tune before he is frightened by a strange voice coming from behind him. He leaps up from his log and runs away. That was all I had to do. From the emotional build-up on the day you'd think I had to play the whole of King Lear.

My mother rose to the occasion, however, by solemnly feeding me a teaspoonful of sugar onto which she had poured a mysterious brown potion. Then she gave me the following sound advice: "When you see the audience in front of you just think of them as a field of cows." Which is more or less what I did – and have tried not to do ever since.

In the event, I sat on my log, remarkably at ease, playing my flute and when the voice sounded my music shuddered to an end in a series of squeaks, as my hands shook, clearly anticipating the invention of method acting. Face contorted with fright, I duly leapt up and ran off to a delicious ripple of audience laughter – music indeed to my ears. I have no memory of the rest of the production, nor of the story. Nor did I come anywhere near to being on stage again for nearly fifteen years. But maybe the moment the cows laughed left a tiny parasite in the brain, waiting quietly for the lights to switch on.

Becoming Acquainted with the God of Light

After a long day's trek through Spanish hills, we staggered into the square of the little town where we'd be staying for the night. In the evening sun, with its trees and church, its two restaurants with alfresco seating under shady canopies, it seemed to be just waiting for our arrival. Our guide smiled happily at our appreciative exclamations, in the middle of which I said to him, "And just look at that lovely lamp-post!"

He looked at me in amused astonishment. "Lamp-post?"

Then he looked more closely. "Why, yes, you're right," he said. "It is lovely."

He laughed. "I'll have to add it to my list of noteworthy attractions," he said.

The lamp-posts of my childhood were dark green cast-iron cylinders, slim, fluted, slightly tapered and ending their upward thrust in a short iron crossbar, sturdy enough to lean a ladder against for servicing the lantern that blossomed above it. They rose from a knee- high, unfluted and marginally broader cylindrical base, in which was set, barely noticeable, a locked door. Once I witnessed a priest of Apollo opening that door to minister to his god's mysteries.

On a dark and smog-filled night they cast a soft and reassuring glow as they guided the wanderer home. I would pause at each one, holding onto it briefly to swing myself round, feeling the flutes play on my hand, absorbing intimations of their history through my fingers – imbibing the strength and power of the Ionic pillars of ancient Greece and Rome in their temples and palaces – a power borrowed by the Victorians in their temples to Mammon. And in some of their lamp-posts.

I coughed in the smog but felt safe and secure with lamp-posts to guide me. If Mammon built them, Apollo felt at home in them. And maybe it was also his music that wove itself into my veins, a melody conjuring melancholy visions of a lovely, loving woman waiting for her lover at night, her face lit under the lamplight – "wie einst Lili Marleen". So it is that countless imperceptible shreds of experience gather together to shape our psyche and move our feet as we dance.

Now I am sitting on the balcony of a hotel in a city in Australia. Its wrought-iron balustrade echoes its Victorian provenance. To my right a supermarket facade weakly mimics elements of ancient Ionic temples. But before me, rising above it all, Apollo has changed his style, shaking off the insults of the intervening heavy-footed concrete and sodium years.

With simple balletic grace he rises, bringing us light lightly, with something of the swan's neck or single stalked flower in the breeze, bending in solicitude over his people; reminding us he is also the god of poetry, music and dance; and as the god of archery he is quietly confident in the sinewy strength of steel.

And a god, it would seem, who enjoys the company of birds …

A Moment of Grace

I was travelling home from London in a train. It was crowded. The carriage I was in was next to the buffet car, so I could see the people queueing. You know what it's like. People squeezing past each other, balancing cans, bacon butties, hot coffee, trying to hold onto passing seats as the train lurches this way and that. Good humoured usually. Comrades in adversity.

The moment happened when the queue was quite long. A young woman was weaving her way through it, clutching cans and cups, held out in front of her, on top of which were perched several triangular packets of sandwiches. Not far behind her came a man similarly laden but with the addition of coffee.

As the woman turned sideways to edge past a particularly bulky customer, bringing as she did so her load over the lap of the seated passenger below her, the train suddenly gave an extra big heave. The man manoeuvering behind her was at that moment for some reason standing on one foot.

Her cans jerked out of her grip upwards, while his launched forwards. Her sandwiches fell towards the seated passenger and the woman opposite him. Their hands reached out, as the man swivelled gracefully on his one foot, hot coffee aloft in one hand, the other reaching for the woman's cans as they descended. He caught one. She caught one and one of his. The sandwiches landed safely into pairs of hands. The other three cans were all caught by others, one-handed, two-handed and in a lap. Not a drop of coffee was spilt, nothing reached the floor and everyone in the queue stayed on their feet. There was a burst of delighted laughter and applause.

That's all – though the afterglow lasted for the rest of the journey. And even as people left the train they parted from each other with a warmer sense of camaraderie than might normally have been felt or expressed. Many of them may have carried the experience home and told the story of it to friends and family.

And why not? It was a special event. A little miracle. There but for the grace of God !… you might exclaim. And what would have happened without it? We'd have collapsed into an untidy heap of bodies, drinks and sandwiches. But we didn't! We defied gravity and kept our balance.

And we did it together, as a group, achieving what the best of ballet companies would be hard put to choreograph and dance after weeks of practice. And here we were, spontaneously dancing our own buffet-bar ballet.

Yesterday

Yesterday today
was still tomorrow.
How could we tell
that the new day
would bring such sorrow

When all promises fade
and ill-judged debts
must be paid
before the final bell?

Time has a way
of warping overnight
snuffing out the light
for those who borrow
and never pay
for what they sell.

For our childrens' sake
let us not sleep
through the guilt
but with them break
habit's toxic hold
so then the story may
tomorrow be told
of how we built
a new day yesterday.

This book is printed on paper from sustainable sources managed under the Forest Stewardship Council (FSC) scheme.

It has been printed in the UK to reduce transportation miles and their impact upon the environment.

For every new title that Troubador publishes, we plant a tree to offset CO_2, partnering with the More Trees scheme.

MORE TREES
LET'S PLANT A BILLION TREES

For more about how Troubador offsets its environmental impact, see www.troubador.co.uk/sustainability-and-community